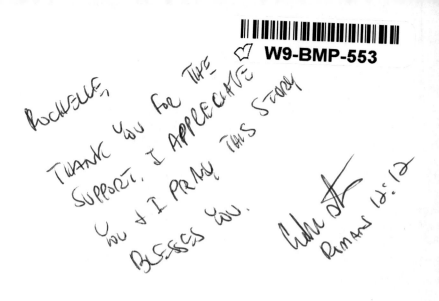

ROCHELLE,
THANK YOU FOR THE
SUPPORT. I APPRECIATE
YOU & I PRAY THIS STORY
BLESSES YOU.

Romans 10:10

Enemy Inside of Me

Enemy Inside of Me

Published by:
NyreePress Literary Group
Fort Worth, TX 76161
1-800-972-3864
www.nyreepress.com

Interior Design:
Devyn Maher
www.doodles.blue

ISBN print: 978-1-945304-97-2

Categories: Christian Fiction

Library of Congress Control Number: pending
Categories: Fiction /Christian Living
Printed in the United States of America

Dedication

This story is dedicated to my wife who continues to overcome her battles with health issues to be a blessing to me and our children.

Alpha

Nyssa walked out unto her balcony. She could feel the warmth of the hardwood deck under her feet and the warm breeze coming off the lake. She closed the sliding door behind her and walked over to her favorite cushioned rocking chair, easing down onto it. She took a sip of her favorite Columbian coffee and savored the dark roast flavor. Nyssa closed her eyes and took another sip before setting the coffee cup down on the table next to her. She took a deep breath and peered at the beautiful blue lake in front of her.

Just like every other morning, it was so calm and peaceful. The morning breeze was barely making a ripple on it. The lake looked like a long sheet of glass as the sun rose over it and the surrounding area. The lake was large—about a half a mile long and fifty yards wide. Being man-made, it wasn't deep enough to boat on, but you could fish in it if you released what you caught. Nyssa loved the fact that she could see different varieties of brightly colored fish as they swam near the top to catch whatever bug had landed on the lake's surface. There were always multiple families of ducks swimming around, and Nyssa would sometimes feed them. She found comfort in having someone to talk to when she was lonely.

One-story lofts, like the one Nyssa lived in, hugged the lake on three sides. They were made of brick and marble, and the color scheme for each loft was unique—no two were the same. All contained plenty of windows, to enjoy the natural light that would shine through. What attracted her to the neighborhood was the fact that the community was all about land conservation. The streets were lined with an abundance of trees, flowers, and shrubbery to enhance the love of nature. Every loft had large solar panels and a small windmill, using the sun and wind as a power source. Together, with the energy from the sun and the wind, enough power was generated to light the entire space throughout the night.

The other side of the lake opened to a large park that had bike trails, walking\running paths, and a sitting area for those who loved to watch the variety of people that frequented the park. Nyssa visited there often to people-watch. She wanted to feel like she was still a part of society, even though lately she had been avoiding it. Every loft that overlooked the lake had the same view, but she rarely noticed anyone on their balcony as early as she was. Nyssa couldn't help but smile, because she was able to wake up to this sight every morning, and she wouldn't dare miss an opportunity to watch the sunrise. Her smile was fleeting as reality crept up and took over.

Nyssa wished for the days when sitting on her

balcony was the beginning of a wonderful day, working in the profession she loved, being with the one she felt she loved, and living in the place she absolutely loved. Lately, her situation was stripping her morning of all joy. At times, she sat out here and tried to focus only on what she saw instead of what was inside her. In those moments, she felt so much gratitude to be alive—overjoyed that she still had a fighting chance to enjoy the life God had given her. Still, in the quiet times, like right now, she felt sorrow.

"God, I am sorry that I cannot appreciate this gift I see daily. You have this here so I can have peace, but all I can think about is my situation and how I still blame you for it." As soon as it rolled off Nyssa's lips, she had to fight back tears. She believed in the power of prayer, and she would pray as often as she could every day. She was just praying for strength and peace with her situation. She always felt better when she had finished praying, but not even a few minutes later, she would fall back into being miserable. She was afraid to feel that way, but it was the truth. She respected God in all his sovereignty, but felt that she was being unduly punished.

In her walk with God, she had always been open about her feelings. She asked for clarity when clarity was needed, or questioned why when things happened that she didn't fully understand. But, this current test had consumed her life and every aspect of her day had become focused on it. Joy could not be found in the things that once brought her happiness and peace. As soon as a moment of peace came, reality wouldn't allow her to enjoy it for long.

She took another sip of her coffee. A few minutes ago, the coffee tasted so good, and she wanted to savor it, but now the brew did nothing for her. She stood and walked to the railing of the balcony, pouring the coffee over the edge. As soon as it hit the lake, it sent a small ripple out that quickly dissipated. Nyssa saw the irony, because that was how quickly happiness left her when she felt it. She had a quick moment of regret over pouring the coffee out, but she shrugged it off. She realized that whatever peace she tried to find out here was now ruined, so she decided it was best to get her day started.

She walked to the sliding door, opened it, and walked into her loft. She was immediately hit with the cold air blowing through the space. Nyssa loved to keep it cold so she could snuggle up like an Eskimo and enjoy a good movie or wrap herself like a burrito in bed. That was the only comfort she enjoyed. Nyssa walked quickly through the living area, kitchen, and den. She eventually made it to her bedroom and approached the nightstand. She picked up a piece of balled-up paper, then began to open and smooth it out. Anger quickly seeped into her mind.

"God why? Why me? Why punish me of all people? There are all types of evil people that spend their whole lives causing pain and misery, but nope... I am the one being punished," Nyssa said, looking up to the ceiling and shaking her head. She had looked at that paper in her hand over a million times over the past three years. It was a significant part of her life and a part she wished she never had to see again.

She read the paper again, as if it was going to read something else. As if what she had read over the past three years was now different. Tears ran down her face. A sick feeling down in the pit of her stomach was accompanied by a strong wave of nausea. She controlled the urge to be sick and fought against what her body wanted to do until the nausea subsided. All that remained was the cool sweat that usually went with being nauseated. Nyssa hated feeling this way, but nothing seemed to stop it from happening.

Usually, when someone gets bad news, over time it eventually doesn't seem as bad as when you first got it. Well, the paper was different. The feeling got worse every time she read it—day after day, month after month, year after year. She kept reading as if she needed it to remind her. The first time she read the paper, it became a memory that would never go away. No matter how hard she tried to forget. No matter how hard she tried to play it off. It was imbedded in her mind forever. Not one day went by without her thinking about and dwelling on it without end. That one piece of paper changed her life tremendously.

She now needed to watch what she ate, and before this, that was never a problem. She was addicted to working out, and still is, but even exercise didn't feel the same. She used to work out because she wanted to. Now, she works out because she must—or, as her doctor put it, because it is in 'her best interest'. She must watch her activities. She can no longer put herself at risk of injury. There were too many precautions to take if that was to happen. She had to be careful with who she was with, which meant they had to know all about her. It was extremely important that they knew from day one to avoid any drama, and there had been drama before. That thought only opened the floodgates and tears came streaming down.

Nyssa looked at the paper and skimmed over it as if she didn't already know what it said. She had it memorized and knew it like the back of her hand—always the same paragraph. She read that paragraph out loud repeatedly when she first received the letter. She just had to make sure it really said what she thought it said, and when it had soaked in, it was too much for her to bare. There were thoughts of suicide and hate for the whole world. All kinds of things went through her mind. But, a cooler head prevailed, and she started praying.

In the beginning, prayer brought peace, but now she felt like she wasn't praying enough because her issue remained, and it was winning. Her prayers were not as wide range as they once were. She would pray for others first, then herself, but now her prayers were self-centered—and for some strange reason, she was okay with that. Nyssa used to feel bad for being selfish. She knew she had much resentment and anger at God. She assumed her prayers were not going to be answered because of how she felt towards Him.

So, she balled the paper back up and threw it on her nightstand. Walking to the bathroom, Nyssa stood in front of the full-length mirror that hung on the door. She let her robe drop to the ground and stared at her reflection. She began with her head. She'd cut off most of the long hair that hung down her back to spite herself for what happened. It now rested at her shoulders. Her complexion was like sand on a beach. With tan, smooth skin, her baby face gave her the look of someone much younger, healthier. A small semi-pointy nose sat perfectly placed between beautiful dark brown eyes. Her petite lips were shaped almost like a cute little letter "M" stretched out above a delicate chin. On most occasions, both men and women approached to compliment her beauty. A few modeling agencies had told her to give them a call, but she never did and never will.

Average shoulders lead to two sculpted arms—not too bulky, just toned enough to confirm to anyone looking that she did in fact work out. She had small hips that many would say were not made for bearing children—too bad Nyssa would never get the chance to find out. She had always considered her legs to be her greatest asset. They were nice and long with toned muscles. She'd turn heads every time she wore a skirt. Being 120 lbs. wasn't bad if it was on a 5'7" frame in all the right places. Nyssa loved the attention and used to crave it. She worked hard for the way her body looked.

As she looked at herself now, she felt like all the work she'd put in wasn't even worth it. She wouldn't be able to enjoy it much longer; the thought of which only brought another onslaught of tears. She was sad and lonely. Anyone looking at her would think, 'if someone as perfect as this is alone, then something must be wrong with her.' In this case, they would be right. There was something wrong with Nyssa.

She had been diagnosed with HIV. For the past three years, this truth had haunted her every day. That was part of the reason she'd kept the test results the doctor gave her. She wanted to have a copy, so that if she ever let her guard down, she could be brought back to reality. Nyssa never thought something like HIV could ever happen to her. But it did, and she can't deny that at all. The medicine she must take every day is an unpleasant reminder. Not to mention her doctor telling her to always check herself for visible marks of advancement from HIV to AIDS. Every sneeze or cough that lasts more than a week was reason enough to go to the doctor. Every scratch or cut she received caused her sleepless nights because she had to watch to make sure it was healing normally. Dealing with this daily was sometimes so overwhelming that it took a good thirty-minute cry to release the sadness, or pity, she felt for herself.

So, once again, her daily ritual was coming full circle. She was at the point where everything else was confirmed by reliving exactly what took place three years ago. She was constantly reminded of the accident that changed her life forever. An accident—not a lapse in judgement on her part. An accident—not her being reckless or careless with her life. An accident—not doing drugs or sleeping around having unprotected intercourse. It was an accident; she was the only one suffering because of an accident that she wasn't even at fault for. She was a victim, but somehow, she was the one paying the price for someone else's negligence.

She could remember some of the events that took place, but there were others that will never be remembered, and she was grateful for that. As she thought about that fateful day, she held back thoughts of being mad at God. She knew that God was sovereign, and who was she to question His plan. Nyssa didn't question what took place; she questioned why she had to be saddled with HIV. Up until then, HIV was her enemy. As a doctor, she'd spent her whole career fighting the disease and counseling those that needed support in dealing with it. There was so much pain in the irony of it all. An enemy she had studied for years. An enemy she knew like the back of her hand. She knew how it was spread, what made it thrive, and what it could do if left untreated. Nyssa knew all of that, but still this enemy lived inside of her, and that was a hard pill to swallow.

Now, as the nightmare flooded her mind, it wanted to be lived out again. It wanted to be replayed repeatedly, and Nyssa did not feel strong enough to stop it from doing just that. Her only hope was that one day, it would stop, and she would be able to get dressed like normal people. She would be able to get up every morning and do a normal daily routine like everyone else, instead of reliving a nightmare as if it just happened. Now, her mind was taking over, and she could no longer focus on getting ready for her day. The nightmare became real again as, in her mind's eye, she could hear the sounds and see the sights of what took place that fateful day three years prior.

"Dr. Thorne, The Swaziland HIV Foundation thanks you for your efforts these past two weeks. Not only did the hospital you are associated with in America give us a large donation, you helped us administer the new trial drug to nearly one thousand children needing to fight the battle of HIV in their bodies. We can only hope and pray that this medicine will give them a fighting chance, seeing that most of them were born with HIV. They need hope that one day they will no longer live with this disease." Mr. Manzini said behind his face mask, as he stretched his green latex hand.

Nyssa wore two gloves on both hands because she was extremely respectful of the virus. She had won just about every award and accolade along the pathway of her career. She was only thirty-four, but very passionate about her job, and she gave more than 100% to her clients, showing maturity beyond her years. She always had a way of saying the right thing and was known for making breakthroughs with patients who were at their wits end dealing with the constant fear of it becoming full-blown AIDS. She made them feel as if a cure was the next dose of medicine away, giving her clients the reassurance of hope. Most counselors walked that fine line between helping and trying to keep their clients coming back by offering only small glimpses of hope.

"Mr. Manzini, don't mention it. I love coming here to help anyway I can. Swaziland is a beautiful place. I love the simplicity of the land. It reminds me of how far removed I am from those that don't live like I do back in the states. It's so humbling to see these people."

"Yes, your dedication to serving here over the last fifteen years straight is so unheard of. Most people find it hard to see the conditions of these people, and how year after year, there seems to be no change in their situation. I remember when you came as a high school student. You were so nervous, but at the same time very curious. I had those same feelings when I was your age, but I was here for a different reason. My uncle was here, and it was a drug addicted lifestyle that forced him to come and receive help. You are here because you truly care and want to be a part of their lives, and for that, I am honored to know you. I am so glad to see you return year after year. I've watched you graduate from high school, then college, and now watch you grow in your profession. You are like a daughter to me."

"Aw, you are so sweet, but don't mention it. Ever since I came on that high school trip, I have been hooked. I remember walking through those doors, scared to death that one touch by anyone with HIV was going to cause me to get it. I tried not to make eye contact with anyone out of fear of being touched. Now, after so many trips here, I have no fear, and all my talks with clients show that they are still human—just like any other healthy person. I feel so bad for those young children. I was expecting to find children sitting down, looking all sad and downtrodden, but they weren't at all. That gave me encouragement and joy that warms my heart. You are also part of the reason why returning is so easy. You feel the way I feel and have the desire to help them as much as I do. Of course, my compassion for these children is at a peak level. They are facing something that no child should ever have to face. They should be running around playing and exploring life to find where they fit in, instead of basically being quarantined and isolated for a disease that many were born with. It really hurts my heart to see them here."

"Understand that everyone appreciates you, and that is why it saddens me that you have to go now."

"I will be back next year, hopefully with more money than this year. Besides, you must keep me posted on your trials and tribulations in the kitchen. I can't believe you're finally learning to cook," Nyssa said with a laugh. "You should have learned how to cook a long time ago, seeing that you are super old."

"Hey! My wife is afraid of me burning our house down, okay. I will make you proud and send pictures of anything I don't burn," Mr. Manzini said, laughing. "Oh bless you, Dr. Thorne. Talking about an old man like that. If I don't burn something, and actually make something edible, I would be overjoyed. Anyway, go to the decontamination station and get your clothes on because your flight leaves in an hour. I look forward to seeing you again."

"Until we see each other again," Nyssa said, giving Mr. Manzini a hug. She knew she was going to miss him. His fatherly touch was something she loved. He'd continued to have an impression on her after all these years because she could hear the compassion in his voice and the care in how he instructed her on things she needed to know. She watched him walk off, then turned to walk down the hall to the nurse's station so they could lead her into decontamination.

As Nyssa walked down the hall, she looked out the window into the courtyard that housed the children she'd administered the medicine to over the past two weeks. They seemed so carefree, playing as if they had no issues at all. They were making the most of the situation they were in. No pity party, and no one feeling sorry for themselves. These children were acting as if they were 100% healthy. They had no fear over whether or not they cut themselves, or the possibility of infecting anyone else, because they all had the disease. The virus was the one common thing that tied them all together. They didn't dwell on their condition, but instead focused on trying to make things as normal as possible.

The Swaziland HIV Foundation had given them a sanctuary to live in. It provided meals, schooling, and shelter from a society that wasn't equipped to deal with the issues that come with HIV. They had doctors, nurses, and teachers supporting the children's every need. These children were receiving medication daily, and that was a luxury they wouldn't be able to receive outside the Foundation. Granted, some of the medicine was a trial formula, and the children were the first ones to receive it, but in the grand scheme of things, they were more than just a victim of HIV; they were part of a process that would help fight, and eventually cure, the disease.

Once Nyssa made it to the decontamination station, she undressed and was checked by the nurse for any scratches or cuts. She was then allowed to shower with a special soap before she got dressed. Nyssa was so happy that she was able to spend two weeks here. This was truly the highlight to her year. The excitement she got knowing that she was coming back to try and make a difference was overwhelming. The couple of nights leading up to her trip every year usually brought sleeplessness due to being so excited. It was almost like a child knowing they were a few days away from going to Disneyland. She loved the way everyone looked forward to seeing her again. They practically met her at the front door, and she felt a sense of belonging and love that made doing her job worthwhile.

Mr. Manzini had been a God-send. He was a slightly built man, but his wiry frame and dark bronze skin gave him a handsome touch that was found in so many men in Africa. He had been instrumental in Nyssa's growth as a doctor and in her overall understanding of HIV. Their discussions on HIV had helped her tremendously in her career, and she knew that she could never repay him for all he had done for her. That was why she made it her goal to get her hospital involved in the outreach here in Africa— not only in helping, but funding the Foundation as much as possible.

Nyssa thanked all the nurses for their professionalism and care as she walked toward the entrance of the decontamination building. She routinely spoke to every one of the nurses and volunteers she made eye contact with. It was just a way for her to show them that she appreciated them and admired all they do. It was not easy working for a Foundation that dealt with such a life-altering disease. She noticed how all the women treated her, as if she was someone special because she was from America. Nyssa didn't want to disappoint them. Many respected the fact that she was a doctor, which for some, was not even an option because of a lack in funds and schooling. Nevertheless, Nyssa didn't want to look down on them. She treated them all with the utmost respect. The way the women carried themselves with so much pride for their culture and African history always made Nyssa feel a little jealous. The rich history of family was still preserved by the fact that they were still here, living on the land they were born on. It had taken Nyssa years of research to truly uncover her history.

Their family history was still being enjoyed as they continued to show their culture by the way they dressed, spoke, and carried themselves. Nyssa laughed to herself, because the way these women wore their hair was just now becoming a trend in America, when they had been doing so for decades—because of tradition, not trend. Their smooth bronze skin seemed ageless. In fact, Nyssa had made the mistake of thinking women were sisters when in fact they were mother and daughter.

Finally making it to the front door, Nyssa was met by Susan Stinson, who was the liaison between The Lonnie Wilson Memorial Hospital in Houston, Texas and the Swaziland HIV Foundation.

"Dr. Thorne, I am here to ride with you to the airport, and I have your luggage here with me as well. We at the Swaziland HIV Foundation appreciate your desire to continue the partnership we have had for the past five years. The efforts of you and your hospital have afforded us a great opportunity for growth beyond our imagination. I hope you have seen that all funds given prior to your visit have been allocated just as we promised. We are now able to offer a level of protection to our staff and volunteers from the same disease they are hoping to cure. We have a state of the art decontamination area, and a new staff lounge and cafeteria to support the needs of our team members. They are grateful to have healthy meals and a place to rest after a long day of work."

"No worries Miss Stinson. We were fully confident that you would use the funds to further the cause. I have plenty of notes and pictures to support just that, and I will share them with my staff back home," Nyssa said as she thought about how she always loved Susan's British accent. Susan reminded her of the fun-loving nannies they had in those hilarious British sitcoms.

"Great, well let's just have a sit here and hope your car will be here soon," Susan said, motioning Nyssa to sit down next to her on a bench outside the Foundation. She sat down and enjoyed the view she had come to love so much. The beauty of the African landscape was picturesque in all its green splendor. The trees were truly amazing to be able to grow in such extreme heat. The story was that the roots ran so deep, they reached water filled with life-growing minerals below. The many colorful flowers that lay across the land looked like paint on a portrait from a distance. The trees provided so much shade that many people built their homes practically underneath them. No two and three-story homes, just small dwellings that were quaint and cozy. The sun was so hot, that the warm breeze only made it seem hotter.

Luckily, Nyssa was used to heat living in Texas. The Foundation was housed on a hill that overlooked a valley, separating the city from the native land. On one side of the valley, you could see a small bustling city with people driving cars, riding on public transportation, or just walking, trying to get to their destinations. The buildings were so much smaller than the buildings in Houston. Most of them still had a 70's look to them. They had pay phones on the side of the road—pay phones were pretty much just landmarks back in the states. The roads were nicely paved, surprisingly, but the pace was still the same. It didn't take more than about ten seconds before a car horn could be heard—usually a newer model car blaring at a late model car that wasn't moving fast enough.

On the other side of the valley, the land before construction took over. There were small villages for many miles. People still dressed to represent what tribe they belonged to. Such a simple living. Many tribes still depended upon the land by farming and growing whatever they were going to eat. They often built wells to keep a steady supply of water available. It was so cool to see them going about their business, not worrying about being on the internet or what the latest clothing trends were. Nope, they were just going about their lives, living exactly like their ancestors.

Unfortunately, somewhere along the line, drugs, alcohol, sex, and diseases had taken over a once bursting scene of city and native land. Nyssa would've loved to say that the tribes were hit less by the HIV epidemic, but she knew she'd be wrong. As much as city life breeds diseases and vices that can bring down nations, a solitary life can make it ten times worse. Dependency on ancestors' stories and remedies have truly doomed a once blossoming land full of culture and pride. Now, the dwindling population was due to the main destroyer of life in this area—AIDS. Most of the tribesman and women had either lost loved ones to the disease or were currently living with AIDS or HIV themselves. That was why it was so important for Nyssa to continue sending money and supplies to the people of

Swaziland to help stop the decay of a people who were using centuries-old methods to fight an ever-evolving disease.

She could clearly see one tribe, huddled around each other as they began to dance. The rhythmic way they danced entranced her. She loved dancing. She would dance for hours on her days off at home. Just loving the carefree feeling it gave her, and how she could look as terrible as ever, but it didn't matter because she was doing what she loved. Now, she watched the tribe move side to side and jump up and down together, all on one accord. The elders danced first to show the younger ones how it was properly done. Age was truly just a number as the elderly men and women jumped up and down with the same effort and agility as the younger men and women. It was so cool to see them dancing in rhythm, and with a sort of childlike essence, they smiled and enjoyed what they were doing. It was so precious to see. Young and old, sharing a dance that had been done for decades, passed down like a great recipe, and never losing its value. Whatever the reason for the dance, they were doing it with full participation and joy.

Nyssa was moved to tears as she realized that some of the same people dancing down there were also being treated for HIV at the Foundation. Worse yet, there were others down there who had refused treatment and were ostracized for that decision. They lived like the homeless, selling their diseased bodies for food or shelter, and getting drugs to numb the pain from the world they were a part of. The city folk, looking for a good time, came to the villages to sleep with the prostitutes—trading money or drugs for unprotected sex. Making a transaction that neither party truly benefited from, the cycle that continued grew the problem daily. Ignorance and a lack of knowledge fueled the spread of HIV to a point of being an epidemic.

So now, the Foundation's mission was to fix decades-old habits and a desire for sex. Some people were okay with rolling the dice and possibly having to live with the disease if they could come and get the medicine for free. It was so sad to see that, no matter if you were in a city or rural country, the disease attacked them both the same. Neither side had put up much of a fight, because the way to win the battle with HIV was protection, and that seemed to be the last thing on the adult's mind as they played Russian Roulette with their health. For the children, there was so much more to it than that. They were either born with it, or infected by a despicable adult raping them. Then, once they had contracted the disease, they were almost immediately shamed and abandoned. Children with no chance of living a normal life. They had to grow up with a disease that was like a ticking time bomb counting down to destruction.

Nyssa's heart began to ache for them. She knew that they were the real reason she returned here every year—to give the children a fighting chance. A chance that was snuffed away by poverty or a lack of morals as bodies were traded for needs, or sometimes just simply wants. Nyssa fought back her tears as Susan interrupted her train of thought to answer her cell phone.

"Oh okay. We will go to plan B. Thank you," Susan said as she put her phone back in her purse. "Small problem, Dr. Thorne. That was your driver. He has two flat tires on his car, but only one spare. I am so sorry. With your flight due to leave in an hour, we don't have time for the company to send another driver, and all of the Foundation's sedans are gone. Are you okay with us taking a local taxi?" Susan asked.

"Um… sure," Nyssa answered reluctantly. She had seen the way taxi drivers drove here. It was like a madhouse on the road with them around, but since Susan was willing to ride with her, she felt a little better.

"Okay great. Let me flag one down." Susan stood up as cars passed in front of the Foundation. Nyssa was happy that many taxis were ignoring Susan's attempts and just sped on by. Nyssa began to think that maybe she would be better off catching a later flight. After a few minutes, Susan was finally able to flag a taxi down. In his haste to stop, he almost caused a three-car pileup. Nothing but screeching brakes and quick maneuvering saved him from being smashed by a car in the front and the back. Susan looked back at Nyssa with a worried expression on her face. Apparently, Susan was having second thoughts as well. Nyssa was going to say something, but was reminded of her boyfriend and how she wanted to get back to Houston because he was waiting on her. Her desire to see him overrode her fears. She was going to ride in this taxi. The driver maneuvered his way into the driveway of the Foundation. He pulled up and immediately jumped out the car, barely giving his car time to stop fully as it jerked when he slammed on the brakes.

"No worries ladies, Ben is always under control," the driver chuckled as he motioned for them to climb in.

"Okay, Ben you said? Be easy with us. I need for Dr. Thorne and myself to make it to the airport in one piece," Susan said as she grabbed Nyssa's hand and walked towards the taxi. Nyssa knew Susan was nervous and needed the comfort of holding her hand. Ben ran around the car to open the door for them. He grabbed Nyssa's luggage and literally threw it into the trunk. Susan sat down first and slid over so Nyssa could sit. She was pleasantly surprised by how clean the taxi was. She had been inside some that were smelly and full of clutter. There were a couple of plastic containers with food in them on the front seat, as well as two folders full of paper.

Nyssa reached for the door handle to pull it closed, but found it missing. There was an arm rest, but it had no padding and a very sharp edge. What gave Nyssa an uneasy feeling was the fact it was loosely hanging on. Ben closed the trunk, then closed Nyssa's door for her. He ran over to the driver side and plopped down in the seat. He immediately positioned the rearview mirror so he could see Nyssa. Then, he put on his seat belt, started the taxi, and peeked back at Nyssa. He reminded her of the guy from the Tom Hanks movie, "Captain Phillips"—the movie where the hijackers took over his ship. Nyssa just wanted to get to the airport. This guy was giving her an uneasy feeling.

"Off we go Ben," Susan said to break his staring contest with Nyssa.

"No worries, Ben is under control. I take you to airport. No worries," Ben assured as he pulled out onto the road, barely checking to see if it was okay for him to do so. Susan looked over at Nyssa and shrugged her shoulders. Nyssa began to pray that they made it in one piece. It was almost comical the way he was acting, but Nyssa didn't want anything to go wrong. The last place she wanted to be was in a Swaziland hospital. All the horror stories she'd heard from people at the Foundation put a heavy dose of fear into her.

"Ben wants to know if you are movie star," Ben asked as Nyssa opened her eyes from praying.

"No sir. I am not a movie star. I am a doctor," Nyssa replied. She didn't want him talking; she wanted him to pay attention to the road because cars were driving erratically around them.

"You look like a movie star. Your hair so long and pretty. You smell like Malva Pudding. My grandma used to make that for me as a kid, and now my wife makes it for me and my five sons," Ben said as he turned around to look back at Nyssa. Susan laughed and shook her head.

"Well, thank you, I guess," Nyssa said, unsure of how else to respond.

"You are welcome Movie Star," Ben said, turning around.

Nyssa was keeping an eye on the road, watching their taxi weave in and out of traffic. They were passing cars on the road, and even going off the road to pass vehicles along the side.

"Ben, we agreed on making it in one piece, remember?" Susan chimed in, double checking her seatbelt. Nyssa did the same as if on cue.

"No worries. Ben is under control. Movie Star, you have a man?" Ben asked, turning around again.

"Yes, I do, and I so dearly want to make it back to him," Nyssa replied with a worried look on her face.

"No worries, Movie Star. I get you home to your man. I bet he loves your long hair. It's so pretty. It's like long goat hair. My father had a goat with black hair so long and pretty. Your hair is pretty like that goat's hair."

"Thank you, Ben," Nyssa said laughing at the thought of her hair being compared to a goat.

"Do you like what you do, you know being doctor?"

"Yes, I love what I do. I love to make a difference in someone else's life. Doing all I possibly can to help them overcome anything they are dealing with," Nyssa answered proudly.

"Ben thinks that is good. Since you like what you do, can you help me with my wife? She nags too much."

"I am not that kind of a doctor. I am an HIV counselor. I help those dealing with HIV, and I help them understand the value of life and how they can still live a full life even with the disease."

"Ben knows why you are here now. You do a good thing Dr. Movie Star. You give hope, and they need it, but my question is, if you had HIV, could you deal with it?" Nyssa was caught off guard by Ben's personal questions. She'd never thought about that before. It wasn't like she was afraid of the virus itself. Sure, she took all the necessary precautions to avoid it, but she had never thought about how she'd react if she contracted it. It was a great question, Nyssa had to admit, so she wanted to think about it for a few seconds; she wanted to give an honest answer.

"Take your time, Dr. Movie Star. That is a great question, and Ben knows this." Ben said feeling confident. "No worries, we have fifteen more minutes until we make it to the airport." So, as Nyssa sat pondering her answer, she watched the road ahead of her. There was a pickup truck in front of them hauling a bunch of trash. It almost seemed impossible for the truck to carry that much trash. As they were driving, small pieces of debris fell off the truck. Nyssa knew she didn't need to worry as long as one of the big pieces didn't fall. She knew they were not far from the airport.

"Tick tock, tick tock. Ben isn't getting any younger, Dr. Movie Star. Answer my question because I have more questions for you."

"This is good. This is like jeopardy. You have to admit, it is a great question." Susan chimed in as she looked over the day planner in her lap. Nyssa knew she was running out of time. She looked out her window and saw more of what Swaziland had to offer. The beautiful coloring of the land looked like God took his time and placed everything perfectly, so you could marvel at how wonderful it looked from a distance. Nyssa could picture herself taking a nature walk out there, just to get a feel for what it would be like to be up close and personal with the land.

"Hey man, you have junk falling off your truck," Ben yelled as he blew his taxi's horn. The truck in front of them had started losing larger pieces of debris. Nyssa and Susan watched intently as Ben blew his horn again.

"Um… Ben, can we just go around him?" Susan asked with concern in her voice.

"No worries, Ben is in control," Ben said trying to reassure Susan that all was okay. The truck's debris shifted, but moved just enough to stabilize itself. Nyssa was watching intently to make sure the straps held the stuff in place. The straps looked like they had seen better days. They didn't seem strong enough to keep the debris contained. There were chairs, tables, trash bags, and a large steel safe all being held together by flimsy nylon straps. Nyssa thought that maybe she should ask Ben to slow down, but they were already going too slow. They actually needed to speed up if Nyssa wanted to make it on time for her flight. Suddenly, a funny feeling came over Nyssa. Something just didn't feel right. Nyssa waited a few minutes until she felt like they were safe again; it didn't appear that anything else was going to fall from the truck. Now, she could focus on answering Ben's question.

"Okay Mr. No Worries, I have a profound answer for you, so brace yourself." Nyssa said, feeling like she was about to give an answer that would satisfy his curiosity.

"Okay, Ben is ready for this," Ben said, keeping his eyes on the road this time, but leaning his head back so he could listen closely. Before Nyssa could answer, the truck in front of them did an evasive swerve, left to right, to avoid a small animal about to run into traffic. That quick motion caused the debris in the back to shift dramatically. The large steel safe slipped through its straps and fell in front of the taxi. Ben had no choice but to swerve to his left to avoid it. Nyssa watched the car barely miss the safe as it bounced passed them in the lane they had been in.

Suddenly, a car pulled out right in front of them, and Ben was forced to slam on the brakes at the last moment. All Nyssa could do was scream before their taxi slammed into the other vehicle. As soon as the taxi made impact with the car, there was a loud boom, followed by crunching metal. Nyssa and Susan screamed above the roar of the wreckage. The front windshield and both windows from the front seat shattered, sending glass everywhere. All the paper and food that was on the front seat flew to the back. Ben turned around right before impact as he tried to hit the brakes, but it was too late.

Ben slammed forward, hitting his head on the steering wheel. He was instantly knocked unconscious as Nyssa watched him flop like a rag doll from the impact. Nyssa hit her head on the seat in front of her, and before she could fall back into her seat, she felt the weightlessness of the taxi beginning to roll over. Nyssa screamed, simultaneously trying not to be sick. Her life flashed before her eyes, and her heart was beating out of her chest. As they rolled over several times, Nyssa and Susan's purse contents fell all around them. Susan was screaming at the top of her lungs, and Ben's unconscious body continued to flop around; luckily still secured in his seatbelt. Nyssa tried to brace herself by putting her hands above her head as they rolled.

Suddenly, Nyssa felt a sharp pain in her side. Every time the car rolled over, she screamed in more pain. After what seemed to be forever, the car finally stopped rolling over, and surprisingly, landed upright on all four wheels. Shattered glass sparkled like diamonds as the sun shone into the car through where the windshield used to be. As the scene grew quiet, the shock of it all set in.

Nyssa felt disoriented as her mind tried to make clear what just took place. The pain in her side was excruciating. It felt as if someone had taken a hot knife and stabbed her repeatedly. She looked down and saw the dangling arm rest impaled into her side—blood spilling from her like a faucet. Nyssa could tell that at least five inches of the metal arm rest had penetrated her side because she could feel the pain into her stomach. Just the thought of having the metal in her body made the pain that much worse. She watched as blood ran down her leg unto the taxi floor. She tried to apply pressure to the wound to possibly slow the flow of it.

What broke her concentration was Susan screaming; her leg was bent in a way that it shouldn't have been bent. Nyssa quickly looked away and noticed Ben, who was now being crushed by the steering wheel pinned to his chest. She began to cry as the scene before her was too much to take in. She knew she was losing a lot of blood, and she couldn't get it under control. The pain from the armrest in her side was too much to deal with. She tried desperately to cling to consciousness as she heard footsteps running towards the car.

Nyssa could faintly hear a beeping sound and people talking. She tried to open her eyes, but couldn't. She felt an oxygen mask on her face for a moment, but soon lost consciousness again. She continued to fade in and out, feeling very groggy. Her body ached, and her head was throbbing. She was able to hear the voices more clearly as she attempted to open her eyes ever so slowly. She couldn't move her neck much, but could see a large, bright light above her. She immediately realized, as soon as she saw five people with surgical masks standing over her, that she was on an operating table. Nyssa wondered frantically why they were operating on her if she wasn't asleep.

She immediately realized that they tried to gas her to keep her unconscious, but it clearly wasn't working. This gas mask was doing nothing more than resting on her face. Her heart rate spiked immediately. Why are they operating on me? What happened? She thought, trying to concentrate and think back as to why she might be in the hospital. She vaguely remembered administering vaccines to the children at the Foundation. She could even remember talking to Mr. Manzini over coffee. Once she felt a small poke in her side, it all came rushing back to her. She could remember riding in a taxi with Susan, then everything went blank, and she couldn't remember anything else. The beeping sound was getting louder and louder, speeding up as the people standing over her looked towards one person standing on her left.

"We need to work quickly here. Okay, we need to get her stabilized again. We removed the object from her side and patched her up, so now we need to start a blood transfusion-fast. She has lost too much blood, and I don't want to lose her," the person-obviously the surgeon-said forcefully.

Nyssa's heart started racing as all sort of questions popped into her mind. She could remember waiting on a car to come pick her up and take her to the airport. She had been with Susan. Wait, where was Susan? Nyssa remembered her getting into the taxi; Susan was sitting right next to her. That annoying driver kept asking her questions.

Where is Ben? Wait, who is Ben? Nyssa thought as the picture became a little clearer. Ben was her taxi drive, and they had gotten into an accident.

"Doctor her heart rate is spiking, we must do something now," one of the nurses said as they monitored her.

"Transfusion now! Bring the blood!"

Nyssa heard that loud and clear, and it was the last thing she wanted to hear. She was in a Swaziland hospital. A hospital in the heart of a city ravaged by HIV and AIDS. She knew, from working with the Swaziland HIV Foundation, that there were two main issues with the hospitals here. One: they didn't have the necessary facilities to properly test all blood they received, and donations were pouring in from people trying to get their hands on the $5 a week payout. Second: there was a staggering number of people who had received HIV from transfusions from tainted blood. Now, here she was, on an operating table, needing a blood transfusion, and she had no way of knowing if the blood she was about to receive was 100% clean. Suddenly, one of the nurses heard Nyssa's heart monitor beeping faster. She noticed that Nyssa was awake and quickly walked over to a machine and reached for a valve. Nyssa could feel a rush of air into her oxygen mask and soon began to drift off.

She tried to scream out that she didn't want a transfusion, but she couldn't say a word. Nyssa tried to kick her legs, but they were tied down, as were her arms. Her eyes opened as wide as they could in fear; she hoped the same nurse would come and look at her again, but she didn't. Nyssa began to feel drowsy, but that didn't stop the tears flowing from her eyes as she realized there was nothing she could do to stop this from happening. She tried to cry out one last time to God, but she was quickly losing consciousness. At that moment, that helpless feeling was all she had to cling to as she fell back into unconsciousness.

Nyssa snapped out of her flashback. Just like every time before, the thought of not being able to speak out and say, "No!" made her cry. Nyssa hated to relive the helplessness of that moment. It was more than a nightmare; it was reality, and it was impossible to fathom. Nyssa looked at her right side, at the scar where the armrest was jammed into her when they crashed into the other car. Susan had to have a hip replacement, but she fully recovered and returned to her job a year later. Ben only suffered a broken pelvis and a few broken ribs. Nyssa was sure he was at home with his wife and five sons, eating Malva pudding, and thinking about the movie star with hair like his daddy's goat. She could make a joke of it now, but when it first took place, she was devastated.

She blamed everyone for what took place. She blamed Ben because of his insistence on driving behind that pickup truck. It was because of him that she had to have a transfusion. She blamed Susan, because if they cared so much about her and the relationship with her hospital, they would have ensured that she had a safe ride waiting before she was ready. She even blamed Mr. Manzini, because if he valued her as a daughter, he would have taken her to the airport himself, like all good fathers do.

And lastly, she blamed God. She had done all that God had ever asked of her. She was making a difference for people with HIV. Where society had given them an hourglass to live by, Nyssa nurtured and gave them hope that the sand wouldn't run out. She cared for and helped thousands of children receive medicine, food, and shelter by donating time and money to the Swaziland HIV Foundation. She worked many long hours and sacrificed many days for others, and never once complained until her accident. But, she was mad at God, and expressed it as often as the anger rose in her.

Even now, she was shaking her head at the thought of God punishing her with HIV even though she had fought against this enemy since high school. God handed her over to the enemy, and she still didn't even understand why. What was also sad was that Nyssa hadn't been back to help in Swaziland since her transfusion and confirmed HIV test. She hasn't had the strength, nor desire, to go back and face everyone, reliving that fateful day. She definitely didn't want to see the place of her accident. Even seeing Mr. Manzini and Susan was too much to think about. They had both reached out, and she replied, but they understood her plight and were offering their support from afar.

She didn't need support. What she needed was to do that day all over again. She would have changed her flight or paid one of the Foundation workers to take her to the airport. Anything would have been better than getting into that accident, needing a blood transfusion, then leaving two weeks later hoping and praying she hadn't received tainted blood. Finally making it back home, she told her boyfriend what had occurred. He'd suddenly had a change of heart about the seriousness of their relationship, and that hurt Nyssa the worst. All the time and effort they put into their relationship, and when the first serious test came their way, everything between them crashed and burned. There was no intimacy, no kissing, and barely a hug from him. He was so afraid of her and the prospect of getting HIV. He never blinked when she was a counselor, talking to people with HIV, or when she invited certain clients over for dinner. He would be cordial, but he never got close enough to touch them.

Once the positive test was confirmed, he ran faster than Usain Bolt. He loved her healthy, but not sick. He wanted children, and there was no way he wanted to have children that had a great chance of being born with HIV. He wanted life the way they once had it, but they both knew it would never be that way again. It was too much for him, so he left. Nyssa wondered why it was so easy for him to just pack his things and leave. He was so quick to delete all social media pictures of them, and quickly changed his status to single. Now, for Nyssa, these past three years had been ones of self-loathing and loneliness. Wishing for the touch of someone else to remind her she was loved. She missed walks in the park and long talks on her balcony. Nyssa knew she was settling with her last boyfriend, but at least she had someone. When friends had get-togethers, and invited her over, she felt better having a man with her, so she wouldn't feel awkward around the other couples. Even though he wasn't her ideal man, Nyssa now felt like he wasn't even worth the trouble, and that stung her through the heart. Now, she watched movies and lived through the imagination of it all. When the movie ended, so did her happiness.

"Nyssa, what am I going to do with you," she said to her reflection as she stepped away from the mirror and walked to the shower. She turned the knob all the way to hot and let the water run for a few minutes until the bathroom was nice and foggy. She stepped into the shower and let the hot water soothe her tense body. Just as she was stepping out of the shower, she heard her cell phone ringing.

"I hope it isn't a client calling me before 8:00 am," Nyssa mumbled. "Hello."

"Hello Miss Thorne. It's Allen from the coffee shop. I was making sure you don't forget your coffee like you have in the past."

Nyssa started to laugh.

"You get free coffee every day, yet sometimes we adhere to your schedule and make your coffee, so it will be ready when you arrive, but sometimes you never show."

"Allen, shut up. I am getting dressed and will be there on time. You are silly and that is also a lie, because I never miss my free coffee."

"Okay, I will take that as confirmation that you will arrive on time. Thank you, Miss Thorne, and I will see you soon," Allen said, trying to stay with his professional tone.

"Whatever, with you talking about, 'Miss Thorne'. I will see you soon. Get off the phone and make my coffee," Nyssa said smiling. The one shining prospect in everything for her right now was Allen. She met him one day in his coffee shop as she was meeting a client there for a session. They stayed way passed closing. Allen was so accommodating, and Nyssa thought that was very sweet. Ever since that night, five months ago, they had been like high school teenagers staying on the phone late and talking about any and everything. She thought it was so cute he was calling her even though he already knew she hadn't missed a morning yet.

Nyssa's only vice was coffee. She would drink at least four or five cups a day. She was glad for her need for coffee because it was a great excuse to see Allen every day. She was starting to like him and welcomed the feeling of getting to know him better, even though she was deathly afraid of him knowing her secret. She pictured him running away or ignoring her phone calls, like some men had done in the past. Nyssa wanted Allen to be different than the rest, but still she avoided any talk of her situation just yet. She was enjoying the feelings she had for him.

"Miss Thorne, I have a question for you. I was wondering if you would like to do something this evening. I have someone closing the shop for me tonight, in case you accept my invitation."

"Oh Allen, I don't know," Nyssa replied as she began to feel nervous about the thought of them being together. As much as she wanted to, her anxiety and fear were making it hard for her to say yes.

"Okay Nyssa. I understand. No worries, I just thought it would be good for both of us to do something besides work for a change."

"Giving up so soon?" Nyssa asked, deciding that she wouldn't let her fear stop her from spending time with Allen.

"Nope, just don't want to talk you into something you really don't want to do. It feels better if you want to go, rather than me begging you to come."

"Begging works," Nyssa joked, laughing.

"I guess I have to humble myself and beg you then. Miss Thorne, will you pretty please come, with sugar on top," Allen said as he laughed with Nyssa. "Come on, do something fun for a change. I want to hang out with you, Miss Thorne, and have a good time."

Nyssa knew he was right. It had been awhile since she'd had any fun. It would be cool to just hang out for once and get her mind off her disease. She was truly just playing hard-to-get because she really wanted to chill with Allen.

"Okay, I will go out. Where do you want to go?" Nyssa asked.

"There is this spot on the beach where they play jazz. They have live entertainment every weekend with great cover bands. The atmosphere is so nice, and most of all, everyone is very respectful."

"Oh, I know that place! That sounds good. What time do you want to do this?"

"Probably about 7:00 pm."

"I will meet you there."

"Bye Nyssa."

"Bye Allen."

Nyssa hung up the phone, then plopped down on the bed. She began to feel sincerely excited; she hadn't been out in a long time, and she wanted to spend time with Allen. But, all that was for later, because now it was time to get dressed. She went to her closet and pulled out her business suit. The one thing that gave her a moment of peace was picking out her suits. She loved wearing business suits and dressing professionally. She loved that, with a suit, came respect; it was another way for her to show the confidence she was surely lacking.

After her diagnosis was confirmed, she told her

clients that she was also HIV positive, and now, her client list had almost tripled. They felt she truly understood what they were going through. She lived in the same prison. She was very busy all the time counseling, but everything she said to give them strength and encouragement, didn't seem to work for her. She couldn't follow her own advice at all, and for that, she felt like a hypocrite. Her words sounded so strong and positive when she spoke them to others. And she could see the power they held by the expressions on her clients' faces as they started to believe. But, Nyssa felt like she needed more.

"Okay, Nyssa, let's go make a difference," Nyssa said aloud as she got dressed, put on her makeup, and put her hair in a bun. Ever since she first started her profession, she always told herself to make a difference. Now, she was making a difference in other people's lives, even though in her own life, she had taken a huge step backwards. So, the only difference she would make today would be to prepare herself to have fun later tonight. Just the thought of going out tonight put a pep in Nyssa's step.

"Oh yeah, she said yes!" Allen announced as he put the phone down and started punching the air victoriously. He kept on punching and punching until he was totally out of breath and had to pause because he felt lightheaded. He let out a deep breath, elated that he'd finally done what he wanted to do. After all these months of waiting, he'd finally gained the courage to ask Nyssa on a date. Many weeks passed by with him planning on asking her, but when a moment would come, he'd freeze up. He'd had so many chances, but just didn't have the heart to go through with it.

When he woke up this morning, he told himself that nothing was going to keep him from asking her. If God allowed him to wake up, then he would do it. He had been pacing the whole morning, just building up the courage to finally ask Nyssa what had been on his heart. He arrived at the coffee shop an hour earlier than usual. The excitement was overwhelming. He thought back to how he had endured five months of conversations, that were friendly in nature, but had a relationship feel to them. He enjoyed getting to know her little by little. Every conversation was so important to Allen, because he could get her to talk about her upbringing and what had molded her into the woman she was now. The woman she was now was who he was currently head-over-heels over. He could tell she was guarded about certain aspects of her life, and he could respect that.

People can only be trusted so much when you first meet them, so it didn't seem strange that she avoided questions when he asked certain things. Allen was good at noticing deception, because as a business owner, he had interviewed so many applicants over the years and learned to catch on when someone tried to hide the truth to make themselves seem worthy of the job. All of that didn't matter right now, because he was happy Nyssa had agreed to go on a date tonight. He knew today was going to be a challenge. He had a coffee shop to run, but his mind was already flooded with thoughts of Nyssa. The past five months had been a blur to him. He got to see her every morning and talk to her almost every night, but tonight was going to be so different. No two-minute chat like they usually did in the morning when she picked up her coffee.

Now, he was going to be with her, possibly sitting

across from her, and the thought of that made him feel a little nervous. Being nervous was a feeling he hadn't felt in a long time. He had to calm down. There were things to do, like going through his mail and placing orders for things he needed in the coffee shop. After having the shop for seven years, he was just now at the point where he was truly making a profit. When he first opened the shop, he had to work another job just to make ends meet. All the money he was making went into expenses. Thank God, he'd saved up money from jobs prior to get him the coffee shop, but that money had been tapped out buying equipment and paying staff. He had started with a clean slate, but had no money to fall back on because every dime was gone, and his bank account was empty.

That was the story of so many entrepreneurs that walk out on faith and start a business with nothing. He was so poor that he basically ate what was sold in the coffee shop. He couldn't afford an apartment, so he slept in his office and used his gym membership for access to the showers. It was a sacrifice that had paid off tremendously, because now he had a grip on his business and was making a considerable amount of money. Competition withstanding, the coffee business was a great money-maker. All in all, Allen knew that he was blessed to have his coffee shop, and for that, he thanked God always.

Even though he no longer had freedom like he once did to enjoy the weekends or take a real vacation, he still loved the time he put in. His hours got longer, and he enjoyed every minute of it. He relished being at his coffee shop all day, every day. Ever since he got up and running, his only goal was to be the best. Allen knew for that to happen, he had to make sure he was doing all he could to separate himself from the major coffee chains. That meant having competitive prices that would draw crowds. He had a vision of where he wanted to be financially, and that served to motivate him.

Allen had a realistic ideal of where he wanted to be every year. As a matter of fact, because he felt so strongly about his vision, everything else was secondary to him. He had gone so far to make sure he was on the right path, that he changed everything about his lifestyle that he felt wasn't going to help him reach his goals financially. He gave up dating so he could truly focus on his shop. Allen knew he had a tendency to give his all to relationships, so he felt it was best to avoid them at all costs—at least in the beginning. Now, he was willing to go against his better judgement for Nyssa. He wanted nothing more than to be with her and was willing to do whatever it took to get her. He could picture himself working less hours and even scaling back so he could spend quality time with her. It was time that he learned to trust, and even depend on, his staff to take his coffee shop to the next level. He didn't have to do everything; a little delegation wouldn't hurt anything. Allen had a wave of happiness come over him, so he sat down in his chair and began to spin in a circle like a little child. He was so excited, he couldn't contain himself.

"Mr. Allen," Emily said as she knocked on Allen's office door. He'd had it closed since he was on the phone with Nyssa. Allen walked over to the door and opened it. Emily always came in to greet him as soon as she made it to work. She was so respectful and considerate of others, and it always brightened Allen's day to see her. She was Allen's first hire, and she was a blessing.

"Good morning Emily. What's up?"

"Good morning. I walked by earlier to speak to you, but your door was closed. I need to know if Nyssa is going to be here at her normal time, so we can have her coffee ready."

"Um, yes, she will be here on time. I was talking to her on the phone to confirm that."

"I like her. She is so pretty. I see the way you light up when she comes to get her coffee."

"Oh, you can see that?" Allen laughed. He knew he wasn't very good at hiding his emotions. He informed all his workers that he would always be the one to give Nyssa her coffee. He made sure he saw her every time she came in; the staff was quick to make fun of him for that. They knew he had feelings for her, so sometimes they would play jokes on him by telling him he'd missed her that day.

"Ha-ha, yes I do see that. You two make a cute couple. I am going to pray that you marry her," Emily said, showing her beautiful smile.

"Oh, please do, and I am serious about that. I mean like every day all day," Allen said with all the sincerity in his heart. He could picture himself marrying her. In his eyes, she was the total package. She was smart, successful, and beautiful—what more could he ask for.

"Let me go make her coffee. You have a great day, Mr. Allen," Emily said as she turned to leave the office.

"You too Emily, and don't mess up my wife's coffee," Allen said, getting a giggle out of Emily.

"Oh, Mr. Allen, don't forget that the museum tour is today, so we need to have a meeting to prepare ourselves," Emily said before allowing the door to close behind her.

Allen had forgotten all about the museum tour scheduled. One of the great things about Allen's coffee shop was that it was literally next to a museum—as the visitors turned to go into the museum, the coffee shop was the first thing they saw. Allen had Emily check the tour schedule every month, so they could prepare for the inevitable rush. He even offered discounts to patrons that brought a receipt from the museum. Allen knew how to get the most out of his location. That was what helped him prosper— his willingness to work with the businesses near him. He offered employee discounts to any business near his shop, so they would support him and spread the word about how accommodating he was. This helped attract new customers that had been referred by an employee of a nearby business.

Allen turned on his computer and looked over his schedule for the day. He couldn't believe he'd forgotten to schedule a meeting with his staff. He was so engrossed in asking Nyssa out on a date, that he'd totally forgotten his schedule for the day. As he looked it over, a reminder window popped up that immediately put a small damper on how he was feeling. Allen's whole mood nose-dived as he was reminded of this anniversary day.

It was nine years ago that he lost his best friend, Nathan. He set the reminder on his calendar so he could call Nathan's mother. His death had been hard on them both. The call was just a way to encourage each other and lend support on this sad day. Allen knew he had about ten minutes before Nyssa arrived to pick up her coffee, so he figured—with his schedule being busy today—right now was the best time to call. So, he walked towards his office door and hung the "Do Not Disturb" sign before sitting back down. After all these years, Allen still remembered the phone number, even though he only made this call once a year.

Nathan meant the world to him. They'd met in high school and had been inseparable since that day. They became fast friends as they talked about the future and how they wanted to own their own businesses. Allen always wanted a coffee shop, which seemed crazy, but he had been fascinated with coffee since he was a little kid. He could remember his grandmother getting up early every morning to make coffee, and the aroma would linger throughout the whole house. He was drawn to the fragrance and the strong flavor associated with it. They would sit down and drink coffee together. She would have a full cup, and he would have about half. It was there that she explained to him the best way to brew coffee, and what true coffee drinkers loved about coffee.

His best friend wanted to open a steak house. His uncle owned a small farm that had a few cows, chickens, and horses. It was there that Nathan learned how to butcher a cow and separate the different sections of meat. Ever since then, he was sure that he wanted to own his own restaurant. So, they began to plan on making the most of their goals by focusing on school and saving their money. That way, they wouldn't have anything stopping them from their dreams. Unfortunately, life had other plans. Allen sat down in his chair and picked up his cellphone, pausing for a second. He was bracing himself for the type of mood Nathan's mom might be in. Sometimes she was calm, and sometimes she was an emotional wreck. Either way, Allen was going to console her to the best of his ability. He dialed her number and took a deep breath.

"Hello Allen," Ms. Watts said, tiredness was obvious in the tone of her voice.

"Good morning, Ms. Watts. How are you doing today?"

"I am as well as I can be."

"I understand that."

"How are you? How is the coffee shop doing?"

"I am doing great, and the coffee shop is profitable, which is always good."

"That is so good to hear. I need to come by there and visit. I keep saying that I will, but I still haven't gotten around to it."

"I understand, Ms. Watts. That is about an hour drive from you. You just let me know when you do so I can roll out the red carpet for you," Allen said, trying to lighten the tone of the call.

"I bet you will. I do want to tell you that I appreciate you calling me every year. It means so much to me that you haven't forgotten Nathan. You were his best friend, and towards the end, you were his only friend."

"Don't mention it. I loved Nathan like a brother, and I miss him every day."

"I do too. I still go into his room, sit on his bed, and pretend that I am talking to him. It brings me so much comfort to do that," Ms. Watts said as Allen heard her voice crack. He knew Nathan loved his mom dearly, and he'd told Allen numerous times that his mom was really his best friend. Allen knew she missed Nathan, because every year, they had the same talk. It was like Nathan had died just yesterday.

"Whatever it takes, Ms. Watts. You do it so you can have peace. Calling you brings me peace and hearing your voice makes my day."

"I love you so, Allen. You have always been like a son to me. I can't thank you enough for being there for Nathan when he fell ill. All the others left him, and no one seemed to care, but you stuck with him all the way until the very end. With you by his side, he could fight longer, and he enjoyed every day. He would always tell me how much it meant that you were by his side."

"Don't mention it. I wasn't going to let him suffer by himself. I made a promise that I would be there for him."

"And here you are, nine years later, still doing what you can for him. Allen, I can only pray that God continues to use you and take care of you by blessing everything you do."

"Thank you, Ms. Watts. Are you going to the grave site today? I know I won't be able to go until later tonight."

"Yes, I am going in a few hours. You take care Allen, and I love you."

"I love you too, Ms. Watts. Bye now," Allen said.

"Bye Allen."

He did miss Nathan, and if he were still alive right now, they would both be owners of their own businesses and would be taking over this block! Nathan was so competitive, and Allen knew he would have challenged him to go after the bigger coffee chains with more aggressive tactics. Allen missed their talks about how to corner their respective markets. Once Nathan got sick, everything changed. Allen saw a side of Nathan he hadn't seen before—fear. He was no longer focused on his goals, but just trying to cope with being sick. Eventually, it consumed him until he wouldn't focus on anything else. That hurt Allen the most, because Nathan was his source of focus at times, and to see him disinterested in his dream was hard to swallow. Suddenly, there was a knock at Allen's door.

"Come in," Allen called as he came back to reality.

"Um… the Misses is here," Emily said as she started to laugh.

"Thank you, Emily." Allen jumped up and followed her out of the office. Allen's heart was racing. This was the highlight of his morning, and he hadn't missed one in five months. As he walked out of the office and into to the prep area, he noticed the normal crowd of regulars. Allen made sure that he made eye contact with everyone and addressed them by name when he greeted them. Emily handed him Nyssa's coffee just as she walked in the door. Allen came out from behind the counter and approached Nyssa. When she made eye contact with him, he wanted to melt. She was so beautiful in her gray business suit. Allen was so impressed, he couldn't believe she was making time for him.

"Ms. Thorne, here is your coffee, and I hope you enjoy it."

"Thank you Allen. It better be delicious, or I'll insist on talking to your manager."

"I am sure you would. Okay, have a great day."

"You too. I guess, I will see you tonight."

"Yes, you will. Have a great day."

"Until I see you again," Nyssa said as she turned to leave.

"Bye." Allen watched Nyssa walk out the door. He was so smitten by her that it took a few seconds for him to get out of the trance he was in. He found her subtle mannerisms so attractive. The way she wore her hair, the way she smiled at him, and the way she walked intrigued Allen to no end. He could find no fault in Nyssa and that made him even happier.

As Allen walked back to the counter, his staff was giggling at him like a group of children. He couldn't do anything but laugh right along with them. He knew he was acting like a little boy with a junior high school crush on the girl next door. Emily gave him the thumbs up, and Allen winked and motioned for Emily and two other workers to follow him into his office for a brief meeting. That left a cashier and three coffee specialists to assist the customers that were currently in the shop. Allen knew his day was going to be busy, but he didn't care because that meant the time would fly by until his date with Nyssa.

"God, why do I feel this way? Why can't I just enjoy this moment?" Nyssa said as she tried to gain her composure. As soon as she drove up and saw the crowd of people, she immediately began to have a panic attack, and for the life of her, didn't understand why it always happened like that. Fear was crippling her, and she was beginning to second guess coming after all. But, deep down inside, something felt different about tonight, so Nyssa was going to go through with this date no matter what it took. She knew she was blessed to even be alive. After seeing pictures from the accident, she couldn't help but thank God for sparing her life—and Susan's and Ben's life as well. It could have been so much worse. God hadn't disfigured her or caused her to lose an arm or a leg, or even become handicapped in any capacity.

No, instead she had a hidden ailment that she was doing a wonderful job of keeping under control with her regiment and lifestyle. Just earlier today, she had received news that her T-cell count was higher than it had been in years—which meant that her medicine was keeping the HIV at bay, so it couldn't advance to AIDS. That was very encouraging news, and Nyssa thanked God for that bit of happiness. She knew she had to make the most of her time; so, she gained control of herself.

"Okay, you can do this. Get out and have fun," Nyssa said, getting out of her car and showing more confidence than she had in a long time. As she walked across the parking lot, she enjoyed her decision to get out of her loft. She couldn't focus at work today because she had been so excited to be going on this date with Allen. Everything just felt so right, and Nyssa knew that, to enjoy herself, she would have to find the strength within to not let her situation get the best of her. As Nyssa walked through the parking lot leading to the beach, she shook her head as she realized she had been sitting in her car for thirty minutes.

She noticed that the place was full of people mingling. The atmosphere felt refreshing as she listened to the cover band playing and took in the beautiful scenery of the beach, coupled with the hypnotic sound of the ocean. Nyssa quickly closed her eyes so she could soak in what she was feeling. She always took a quick moment to take in all she could see and hear, because it always seemed to have a calming effect on her. She opened her eyes and marveled at how the beach was lighted perfectly. The perimeter of the restaurant was impressive, as it took up a large portion of the beach. There were light poles along the sand on all four sides so you could see the entire area. The brightness of the lights made the backdrop of the ocean that much darker. There were wires tethered to each pole to connect one to the other, and light bulbs every twelve inches that made it look like a well-lit spider web.

There was a large area made specifically for dancing. Two sections of fifteen tables lined either side of the dance floor. The third side was where the cover band was playing and behind that was the kitchen, a large wine rack, and restrooms. Behind the band lie the beach, with a long sidewalk running parallel to it. Couples were already dancing, and that made Nyssa jealous. She wished she was out there dancing, and truly enjoying the night, versus fighting a panic attack. She was so nervous, she could feel her heart beating in her throat. The sensation was accompanied by a nervous sweat. She hoped her body language didn't show how nervous she truly was.

She felt so out of place even though, at one time, this was her type of place to chill. It was amazing how a hidden disease could take away all joy—just by its presence. As Nyssa looked across the beach, she felt as if she had a bright, blinking neon sign over her head announcing to everyone that she had HIV. She wasn't sure if it was just her or what, but it felt like all eyes were on her. Every time she made eye contact with someone, it felt like all her secrets were being revealed—like they were watching her every move. Logically, Nyssa knew it wasn't true, but the feelings were still tough to deal with.

These were the same feelings her clients spoke of when they went out in public. It was the paranoia of having a deadly secret, and those around you having no clue, so you worry about what they think or what they would do if they found out. Would they all point and laugh? Would they run away and hide from her? The paranoia was playing tricks with her mind. Nyssa wanted to enjoy herself so she fought the desire to go back home or to sit in her car and hide.

"Okay, where are you at Nyssa?" Allen whispered to himself as he found a table. He had waited in his car so he could walk in with her when she arrived, but he was worried about not being able to find a place to sit. This place filled up so fast on Fridays, and there was no way Allen was going to make Nyssa stand the whole night. So now, his head was on a swivel, trying to see when she walked up. Looking around, there were so many beautiful women out tonight. So many clusters of women together at tables, possibly looking for a man. Allen felt in his heart he was going to be with the most beautiful one of them all. In his mind, Nyssa was second to none, and he knew that these women couldn't possibly compare to her.

Trying to spot Nyssa was going to be harder than Allen expected. This place didn't technically have one way in and one way out. It was on a beach, so you could come in from all directions. The only thing that could be called an entrance was the path from the parking lot. He was so excited to see her. All day long, his mind thought of what he would say and how he would act around her. His goal was to be relaxed and calm. Allen wanted to be respectful, but at the same time, express his feelings for her. He gave plenty of hints in their conversations on the phone, but tonight he wanted to be blunt and straight forward.

He wanted to be in a relationship with Nyssa;

he'd had visions of what it would be like. Holding hands, conversing, and spending time together flooded his mind constantly. It was like he'd had an out of body experience, because he didn't get overwhelmed by the rush at the coffee shop today, like he normally would have. Granted, the crowd was one of the largest the shop had ever served, but it didn't seem to faze him at all. They had to work at a fast pace just to keep the line from being out the door. He hadn't had time to eat or relax all day long. Once he had finally gotten over the wave of customers, and it was getting to a point where his staff could handle things, he ran home, showered, and came straight over.

Not only did he have her on his mind, but Nathan as well. Allen didn't have time to go by the gravesite like he had the past nine years. This was the first year anything had ever come before his visit. Allen knew he was going to enjoy every second of Nyssa's company tonight, and there would be no way he was going to rush this date to be over. He felt selfish for feeling that way, but deep down inside, he knew Nathan would want him to enjoy himself. After all, Nathan loved the ladies, and he'd found time for relationships when Allen hadn't. That was one thing about Nathan; women were his weakness. He wanted to be a good guy, but his eyes couldn't be tamed. He was so much like Sampson, from the bible, that it became his nickname. Allen would call him Sampson every time another woman caught his eye. He loved to brag of his conquests, and Allen knew how to tune him out when he was speaking of them.

Allen often wondered what Nathan would think of Nyssa. He knew she was the type of woman Nathan liked. Allen had to shake that thought and just focus on the fact that Nyssa was going to spend time with him.

No competition from Nathan was going to stop him from enjoying this night. Even if he had to leave his staff at the coffee shop to fend for themselves. There was no way he was going to cancel this date. Not even his momma calling and telling him she was making his favorite gumbo. Nope, not even that was going to stop him from being here tonight.

Allen went through so many outfits. He wasn't sure if he should get dressed up with a suit, or dress casually with jeans and polo shirt. He just stuck with jeans and a dress shirt. He didn't want to do too much, but at the same time, he wanted to impress Nyssa. Allen began to focus even harder on finding her, since it was now a few minutes past 7pm. Finally, he noticed her standing where the sand and sidewalk met. He shook his head because she looked so pretty. He was amazed every time he gazed upon her. Allen got up and walked over to her.

"Hello Miss Thorne," Allen said snapping Nyssa out of her thoughts. She jumped at the sound of his voice, but that made her smile. If anyone could help her with her nervousness, it was him.

"Hey Allen. You scared me," Nyssa admitted as she gave him a hug. She caught a whiff of his cologne and loved it! She thought it was crazy that this was technically their first embrace. After five months of talking almost nightly on the phone, and seeing him in his shop daily, that was the first physical contact they had ever had. In an old-timey way, Nyssa thought it was romantic. "Wow, I was just caught up in the ambiance of this place."

"Sorry about scaring you, that was my bad." Allen felt bad about scaring her, but felt great about finally hugging her. "Yes, the ambiance of this place is awesome, and you best believe this place always attracts a nice crowd.

Good thing we arrived early, because in a few hours, it will be totally packed... almost standing room only. I must say, you look so beautiful. In my opinion, I definitely have the finest date out here tonight." He was proving to himself that he was going to be more straightforward with his feelings. As confirmation that he was making the right choice, Nyssa began to blush.

"Oh, we are on a date huh?" Nyssa said, winking at Allen to let him know she was playing. "I am really happy you asked me to come. It has been too long since the last time I got out my loft to do something I enjoy."

"Good, well let's go to our table. I have one right over here," Allen said, escorting Nyssa through the crowd of people. They had a table near where the band was playing. Allen pulled out the chair for Nyssa, as a true gentleman would. He sat and immediately couldn't stop smiling. It had been awhile since a man smiled at her like that. She remembered how her boyfriend smiled like that when they first met, but after the first year, he became comfortable, and the relationship grew stagnant until he finally left. Nyssa was glad he was gone, because now she had an opportunity to get to know Allen.

As she was looking at him, she began to see small characteristics that made her like him even more. She loved his preppy look that he wore so well. How he always had a fresh haircut and how his glasses always matched whatever color he was wearing. How he wore the right colors to accent his dark brown skin, and the way his clothes fit his slim frame just right. He dressed nice enough so you knew he took pride in how he looked, and Nyssa loved that. Allen looked so handsome, and the way he carried himself made him even more appealing. She liked how he was always respectful of her and other women. Nyssa watched him at times in his coffee shop as he helped the female customers. He always made sure they had his attention, and he was a great listener, even when they rambled on about coffee flavors. Even now, he was giving her his undivided attention, and there were plenty of pretty women out here tonight showing enough skin to make men look their way. But, Allen's gaze stayed locked on Nyssa, and she liked that.

Here she is, sitting across from him after all these months of conversations on the phone. What made her the most nervous was their conversations on the phone were always in a controlled environment. She could pick and choose what to talk about, and when it was something she felt led to a topic she didn't want to address, she could simply come up with a reason to get off the phone. Sitting across from him was making her feel trapped; she was starting to feel another panic attack coming on.

"Honestly, you look like you could use a drink," Allen said as he motioned for the waitress to assist them. "No offense."

"None taken. I could use a drink. Right about now, that would be the best thing for me," Nyssa said, hoping it would help her relax.

"I'm not going to lie, but I need a drink too. I am a little nervous being with you right now. I have been waiting all these months to go out with you, so I think I need a little liquid courage as well." As soon as Allen said that, Nyssa's heart jumped. She felt the same. She liked how open he was to talk about how he was feeling. As a counselor, Nyssa always instructed her clients to say exactly how they were feeling so she could pinpoint what was truly going on with them. Most of her and Allen's conversations on the phone consisted of him talking and her listening. But even then, Nyssa noticed how Allen was honest with his feelings. He made it known, in about a month, how he felt about her. He would always drop subtle hints about his feelings for Nyssa. He would never come on too strong, but always mentioned it at the right time to keep Nyssa enjoying his conversations.

"Yes, how may I help you tonight?" the waitress asked. Her body language made it clear that she did not want to take their order, or even to be working at all, tonight.

"Are you okay with wine, or would you like something stronger?" Allen asked, hoping that she'd go with the wine.

"Oh, white wine is perfect for me. Thank you."

"Okay, Miss Thorne wants white wine, so let's get a bottle," Allen said looking over the wine selection on the menu before pointing out the one he wanted to the waitress. She walked off, and Allen took a deep breath, still smiling at Nyssa. If this was all they did all night, he would be totally content with that.

"A bottle? What kind of girl do you think I am?" Nyssa asked, laughing.

"Well, if I thought you were an easy one, I would have gotten something stronger. I know for a fact that white wine relaxes me and helps me with my nerves."

"You must have a lot of nerves to be needing a whole bottle."

"If you only knew, Miss Thorne… if you only knew," Allen answered as they both laughed. She had to pinch herself to make sure this was happening. She was on a date and was glad she hadn't made up an excuse to not come.

"So how was your day today?" Allen asked to break the silence.

"It went well. Today was quiet and mundane. I saw a couple of clients, shopped a little, and before all of that, my stalker called me early this morning. Get this, he literally begged me to go out with him."

"A stalker, wow. I guess I have underestimated how irresistible you really are," Allen said laughing at her comment. He did feel like a stalker at times, as he always called her the same time every night and would want to call her right back if they had gotten off the phone early.

"Obviously. You need to understand who you are dealing with," Nyssa said, as she knew he couldn't possibly understand what she truly meant by that statement. He knew about her family and how she grew up in a single parent household with her dad—because her mom decided she wasn't fit to be a mother. Her dad made sure she had everything she needed, and he put her in one of the best private schools in Houston. It was there she had the opportunity to travel and where the seed was planted on her mission trip to Swaziland to help those with HIV. That he knew. What he didn't know was what Nyssa was afraid of him finding out.

"So, what was your day like today?"

"My day was fulfilling as I was able to have one of my most lucrative days in a long time. We had more than a couple tour buses come today. With my coffee shop being near a museum, we get a lot of tours coming through, and today we were busy since right after you left until I was finally able to leave so I could freshen up for tonight."

"You freshened up? Can't tell," Nyssa joked. She found herself being silly, but very comfortable, with Allen.

"Wow. Okay, you got me. You are silly, and I like that about you. I am going to be honest with you, when you told me you were a doctor, I was worried about us not being compatible."

"Really? I am glad we are compatible. I love our talks and all of the things we have in common," Nyssa said as the waitress brought their wine.

"Excellent," Allen murmured as the waitress poured some wine into the two glasses she'd brought. She then set the bottle down and abruptly walked off.

"Okay, I guess we don't need anything like an appetizer to nibble on," Nyssa quipped.

"Obviously, we don't need anything else. Okay, can we toast to our first date?" Allen said as he raised his glass.

"We sure can, when we finally go on our first date," Nyssa said, being silly.

"Okay, you have all the jokes."

"My bad. Yes, let's toast to our first date," Nyssa said as they touched glasses and enjoyed a sip of the wine. Nyssa knew Allen would take a modest sip, but she took more of a gulp to calm her nerves.

"Okay, is there something I need to know?" Allen joked as he watched Nyssa drink her wine like it was water. He'd had that exact same thought, but didn't do it.

"Ha-ha, not really. If my car starts up, then I am good. The court told me how much wine I can consume to stay legally sober. If I stay below that, then I am good," Nyssa replied with a straight face. Allen was totally fooled.

"I don't know what to say..." Allen admitted, looking a little confused. That came out of left field, and he wasn't ready for it at all.

"I am only playing, Allen. I don't have one of those things in my car. I'm not an alcoholic."

"See, I told you I am nervous and here you are

confusing me. I didn't know what to say because I really like you, and I had no comeback with that one."

"I get silly when I'm nervous, that's why I need this wine to kick in so I can just be me."

"Oh this, isn't you? I like you being silly though. That is a great balance to me because I am normally even-keeled. I try to have fun, but I sometimes overthink situations and that can take all the fun out of what I'm doing."

"I am silly most of the time, when I'm not feeling sorry for myself."

"Why are you feeling sorry for yourself?" Allen asked with an intrigued look on his face. Nyssa hated that she let that slip. She knew she needed to be on her best behavior to keep her secret a secret until she was ready to reveal it.

"You know, long hours and not really doing much at all except working out," Nyssa said to clean up the mess she almost made.

"You work out too. I try to go to the gym at least twice a week."

"That is not working out. If you are only going twice a week, then you are just visiting the gym," Nyssa said as she busted out laughing.

"Ha-ha, now that might be true. I was stretching the truth anyway. It's more or less twice a month, not a week," Allen knew that was definitely closer to the truth because he hadn't been to the gym in a minute.

"I can tell you only go twice a month. My arms look better than yours," Nyssa said as she flexed in her sleeveless blouse, showing off her chiseled arms. "Just kidding, I love working out. It's a bit of therapy for me."

"You do have nice, sculpted arms, and that is the

second time you have said something like that. Are you being silly, or is something really going on with you?" Allen asked. Nyssa wanted to physically kick herself in the butt. She lost focus that fast, and if she slipped up like that again, she'd have to let him know.

"You know how crazy this world is. So much drama and evil happening daily. It gets overwhelming when you watch the news or read an online newspaper," Nyssa back-peddled, trying to divert the talk from a personal note to a more general one. She hated lying to Allen, but she had no choice. She was nowhere near ready yet. Allen was immediately impressed with her. She had compassion, and he loved that about her.

"You too? I pray for this world. I am so afraid of what this place could be like ten years from now. So, what I do is live each day like it is my last, because you never know. I refuse to not enjoy all that God has given me and allowed me to do. Think about this, I get to wake up every morning healthy and fully functioning. I thank God for that. So many people had plans to wake up this morning, but didn't, and I did, so that motivates me to always make the most of every day," Allen said genuinely as he took a sip of his wine. He truly felt that way because of what he'd endured watching Nathan waste away while he was sick. Nathan had so many regrets, and there were days when all he would say was how much he wished he could this or that over again.

Nyssa reflected on Allen's last comment. It resonated deep in her mind as she knew she should be the one thinking and living that way too. HIV may not be the death sentence it once was, but she should be trying to live out each day as if her time was short. Instead of hiding and feeling like life was already over, she should be truly trying to enjoy the blessings that God has given her, instead of being angry with Him.

"Well, here is to living every day like it's our last." Nyssa lifted her glass to Allen's. Nyssa finished her wine, and it felt so good going down. Allen recognized that she was finished and poured some more in each of their glasses. The music, the scene, and the company was making Nyssa's heart flutter. She so missed things like this as she sat in the prison she's made for herself. The prison she'd wasted the last three years in with her own personal pity-party. All those nights, she could have been here with Allen enjoying accomplishments and making memories, instead of crying herself to sleep, feeling sorrow and despair, even though there was still hope for a full life. Having Allen in her life to put things into perspective was giving Nyssa hope she had truly been lacking.

"So, we better get something to eat or we will both be passed out on this beach in a minute or two." Allen gestured toward the already half empty bottle.

"I am good. I ate before I came." Nyssa was lying again, but she didn't want anything to slow the wine from going into her system. She wanted to be mellow, and she knew the wine would help.

"Alright. I know you are off tomorrow, but I have a coffee shop to run. Last thing I need to do is stumble in there with a hangover." Allen couldn't recall the last time he'd had a hangover because it had been awhile since he last drank any alcohol. Saturday mornings were extremely busy for his shop, and he knew how much harder it would be to work and not be 100%.

"What do you mean? White wine does that to you? Come on Allen, put your big boy pants on. Don't you have your own coffee shop? You have a ton of coffee to help you with your hangover. Don't be a wimp," Nyssa said, poking fun at Allen. She liked how conservative he was, because normally she was too. But, tonight she was trying to ease the uneasy feelings she had about being out in public.

"Well I am trying to impress you more than anything else. I want you to like me, and I definitely don't want to do anything to make you see red flags," Allen told her as he took a sip of his wine.

"If you want to impress me, then you keep on doing what you're doing. I love honesty, and when you are 100% truthful with me, then I will trust you and open up more." Nyssa couldn't think of anything more hypocritical than her last statement. Allen could bare his soul right now, and she still wouldn't tell him the truth about her HIV diagnosis. She wouldn't let that reality ruin this moment. No way, no how.

"Don't worry Nyssa. I will be honest with you, because I so dearly want you to trust me. Ever since that first night I laid eyes on you, I have totally...wait, hold on a second..." Allen paused as he filled his glass up to the top, then gulped it down real fast. Before he made it half way, he had to stop because he started to laugh. He couldn't believe he did that, but it was too funny for him to go through with it.

"That's what I am talking about! Yes, loosen up and make a fool of yourself." Nyssa laughed with him. He totally caught her off guard with that, but it was funny nonetheless.

"I need something to give me the courage to say what I am going to say. I have no clue how you are going to take it, so I can always blame the wine," Allen said, wiping his eyes from laughing so hard.

"I guess you are going to say something earth shattering, since you are drinking like that." Nyssa shook her head at Allen who was still trying to calm down from his fit of laughter. Nyssa really enjoyed that moment. He was being himself and seemed to be so much fun.

"Not really earth shattering, but the truth." Allen wanted to totally confess to her his true feelings, but didn't want to come on too strong. So, he knew he better dial it back a bit.

"Okay, I will take that as well, but it better be good, and I better like it," Nyssa said jokingly.

"Okay, I was saying that ever since the first night I saw you sitting there in my coffee shop, I was blown away. In all my years living, I cannot recall a more beautiful woman. I was standing there watching you, and I was literally mesmerized. I didn't want you to leave, and the later you stayed, the better because that gave me a reason to talk to you. When I walked over to your table, I was so nervous, and when I peered into your eyes, and you smiled at me, I was hooked. I couldn't focus the rest of the night."

"Really? Allen that is sweet." Nyssa thought it was so cute of him to say that. She really needed to hear it, too.

"I am telling you, I thought of you that whole night, and when you started to come in on a regular basis, I was ecstatic." Allen looked deeply into Nyssa's eyes. She felt the truth in his words and melted at hearing it.

"Well, I am going to be honest with you. Free coffee helps because I am addicted to it. Keep giving me free coffee, and you will see me every day," Nyssa said as she smirked. She wanted to let him know how she felt, but she was afraid to go down that road without telling him what he didn't know.

"Hey, I have no problem supplying your coffee. Seeing your pretty face every day is more than enough payment. I consider that an unfair trade, honestly, because I come out on top on that deal."

"Oh, don't worry. Wait until the next date. I will make you back up that statement. No, I am just playing." Nyssa hoped there would be plenty more dates. If Allen was going to be this open with her, then she wanted to hear what he had to say. Nyssa loved to hear him say what he remembered from that first night. For her, it was different because she was talking to a client, and she was so totally focused on the client's issue, that she didn't see or hear anything else.

The client was speaking about how tough it was to date with HIV, and Nyssa knew that too well. She could still remember when she had the courage to date a couple of times. One date, she was with a guy that seemed really nice. Nyssa used to tell guys early on that she had HIV so they wouldn't trip on her. They were talking about life, and she felt it was a good time to tell her date about her predicament. He had just explained how compassionate he was with those who were less fortunate or who he felt were dealt a bad hand. To Nyssa, it was a perfect segue for what she was about to mention. So, she gathered the courage to tell him she had HIV, and the look of disgust on his face made Nyssa want to run and hide. He was so upset that he stood up and made a scene. He called her all kinds of names and stormed off leaving her sitting in the restaurant until she had enough courage to walk out. She cried the whole way home, and that entire weekend she was no good to anyone. That was the second-time honesty was met with embarrassment, and ever since then, Nyssa wasn't going to say anything unless she had to. So, when her client was speaking of a similar situation, Nyssa understood fully.

"If we have another date, I will pay whatever it takes, well maybe... within reason," Allen said, catching himself before he dug a hole he couldn't get out of.

"I'm glad you cleaned it up because I am a doctor, and I have very expensive tastes. No, I'm just playing. Being a doctor has afforded me the ability to get all I need and more, so you are safe," Nyssa said as she sipped more of her wine.

"For you, who knows what I would do." Allen took a sip as well.

"Okay, let's see what you would do for me. Let's do shots." Nyssa motioned to the waitress that was walking around with a tray of shot glasses.

"Shots? You don't want me to go to work tomorrow."

"I recall you saying, 'live everyday like it's your last'. Put your shot where you mouth is," Nyssa said in a matter-of-fact tone.

"Wow, you are using my own words against me. Okay, let's do it," Allen agreed as the waitress dropped off two shots. Allen knew he couldn't back down now, and a part of him was loving what they were doing, so he went with his feelings. They both looked at each other and raised their glasses. They nodded and drank the shot together. As soon as the shot went down her throat, Nyssa knew she shouldn't have done it. It had been years since she had consumed this much alcohol in one sitting. The buzz she was beginning to feel was real and should have been expected.

"Okay, I don't normally drink like this. I just hope I don't pay for it later," Allen said, smiling and shaking his head at Nyssa.

"Me either, we will either remember this night for being silly, being buzzed, or being sick tomorrow."

"Right, and I hope it's not for being sick because that is not an option for me."

"If you are sick tomorrow, I got you," Nyssa said with a sneaky smile on her face.

"So, you would take care of me, Nyssa?" Allen asked.

"Um no. I would go to your coffee shop and do your job, only better."

"Really?" Allen said as he started to laugh. "You are crazy."

"No, I would take care of you… if I'm not sick."

"So, as pretty, silly, and cool as you are, I'm wondering why you are not with someone right now. It's not like you don't have many options when it comes to dating."

"Surprisingly, I don't have any options. I haven't dated in a long time. How about you?" Nyssa asked to direct the attention away from her.

"I haven't dated in years either. Just so busy with my shop and trying to make the most of it. I hate failure, so I am doing all I can to ensure my coffee shop is a success. But still, me being single is one thing, it's hard to believe you are single," Allen said as he stared at Nyssa. He didn't want to think there was something wrong with her, or that she was crazy, or anything close to that. His hope was that she too was so consumed in her work that she didn't have time to date.

"It happens," Nyssa said. It was moments like this when she wished she didn't have HIV. This night would have been so much more special if she was disease-free. She could let her hair down and be herself. She knew Allen was searching for the truth, so she needed to take control of the situation. She was feeling the effects of the white wine and the shot heavily.

"Well, do you want to take a walk?" Nyssa asked. She wanted to take control of this night to protect herself. She liked the atmosphere, but she also wanted to walk along the beach and listen to the ocean. Allen looked at Nyssa for a moment and nodded.

"Well, I am going to bring this bottle of wine with us so we don't waste it."

"You are trying to get me drunk. Let me carry the bottle in case you get frisky, then I can bust you in your head. While walking, be on your best behavior because you might want this doctor, but you will be needing another type of doctor if you get out of line." Nyssa joked as she stood up and waited for Allen to do the same.

"Oh wow, no pressure on me at all then." Allen handed the bottle to Nyssa, who started to drink the rest of the wine right out of the bottle.

"Really? See I was going to do that, but I was too scared." Allen took the bottle from Nyssa and finished off the rest.

"What we look like drinking straight from the bottle?" Nyssa asked, laughing hysterically.

"I tell you what we look like. We look like a couple of lushes," Allen said.

Nyssa wasn't going to focus on what anyone else thought at this moment. The buzz she was feeling was allowing her emotions for Allen to take over. Nyssa reached out her hand, and Allen grabbed it. She could feel a chill go up her arm. The comfort of his hand holding hers, and the way it was so tenderly done, meant the world to her.

She hadn't held a hand that was connected to someone she thought was special in a long time. She didn't want to let go, and as a matter of fact, she was content with just holding his hand. You never realize how much you miss something until you stop doing it. Holding hands was such a simple gesture, but when you haven't done it in a while, you forget how special it is, and Allen's firm grip assured her he felt the same.

"Let's go." Nyssa pulled Allen towards the sidewalk along the beach. It was a path that many people were already walking from one side of the beach to the other. The sidewalk was made of sand, and it was smoothed out, so you could tell it was made to be a path. Nyssa bent down and took off her sandals so she could feel the sand under her feet. The sand was so soft and smooth to the touch. She put her shoes in her left hand and grabbed Allen's hand with her right.

Allen loved holding her hand as they walked down the beach. They passed by so many couples walking along the path. Some were just looking at each other lovingly. Some were deep in conversation, and the world meant nothing to them as they conversed.

"Thank you for asking me to come out tonight."

"It was my pleasure. Besides, I have been wanting to ask you for months now."

"You big fraidy cat. Months? Really?" Nyssa said giving Allen a hard time.

"Whatever. I am only able to do what you allow me to do. Stop giving me a hard time and make it easier for us to get together." Allen knew he wanted that more than anything else.

"I will do better from now on. Let's just plan on

doing more of this." Nyssa smiled at Allen. She felt so genuinely happy and was thanking God for allowing this night to take place. For this night, she was totally free. Free from her pity-party, free from everything that reminded her of her condition. Her mind was truly on the moment. And what a moment it was for Nyssa! It was almost as if this was her first-time ever being on a date. She had so much excitement and enthusiasm that it was all-consuming.

Nyssa closed her eyes and could still hear the band playing behind them and the ocean making music to their side. Along the path they were walking on, they had speakers every twenty feet so they could still enjoy the music playing from the restaurant. It played softly in the background of their moment. In Nyssa's mind, she could see every note as it surrounded her. The night breeze blew through her hair, just cool enough to give her a romantic vibe. In her heart, Nyssa was free from it all, and a simple act of hand-holding calmed her nerves and gave her confidence.

It was moments like this that Nyssa knew God was still there for her—as if this night had been tailor made for her. What could be more needed than a night like this for her to know that there was hope? This night wouldn't take away the HIV, but it would help Nyssa understand that life was still enjoyable. Why she let the disease kill her joy daily was something Nyssa couldn't understand, but if more nights like this were in her future, she was going to stand up to the disease no matter what it took.

"I can't get over how pretty you look tonight. I knew you were going to be, but it seems like every time I look at you it's the first time. I have felt this way since the first night I met you, and it hasn't wavered at all."

"I love when you say that. You make me feel so

special, and I love it. I want you to know that I really like you too. I know I have been sending mixed signals, and not really committing to say how I truly feel, but rest assured Allen, you have my attention and my feelings are for you."

Allen felt so relieved that all these months of wondering if Nyssa liked him, or if he was forever stuck in the "Friend Zone", were finally over. She was letting him know she liked him. He felt like taking off running across the beach, shouting his happiness for all to hear.

"I promise you that I will not make you regret being with me. I will do everything I can to make you as happy as you deserve to be," Allen said, kissing the back of Nyssa's hand.

"I have no doubt about that at all. I have listened to you over these past five months. You have not wavered in your feelings for me, your desire to go out with me, or your patience with me keeping you at an arm's length. You have respected my privacy, and you didn't get mad no matter how much I kept my guard up." Nyssa squeezed Allen's hand tighter to let him know she enjoyed holding it.

"I am willing to do whatever it takes to continue reassuring you that I will never change, but will only try to be even better for you." Allen knew that was his sales pitch. That was the statement he felt would hopefully seal the deal with Nyssa.

"If you live up to that last statement, then we will have plenty more days of enjoying each other."

"Oh, would I like that."

Nyssa would have paid to hear Allen say that. In her three years of loneliness, she wondered if anyone would ever want to be in her company or tell her that she was important to them. Allen was saying all the things Nyssa wanted to hear, and she was hooked on hearing more. As they walked further, they came up to a twenty-foot-long wall that was made for people to sit on or lean against if they were tired or just wanted to chill.

"Hey, do you want to go over and sit on the beach behind the wall?" Nyssa asked as she pulled Allen in that direction.

"I think you have already decided for us, since we are already headed that way." Allen chuckled, willingly following her. They walked off the path and started walking on the beach. The sand was much thicker. Their feet dipped to their ankles every time they took a step. They made their way to the wall and sat down on the sand with their back to it. Along the top of the wall was a row of lights, and you could turn a bulb if you wanted light or turn it the other way if you didn't. Nyssa turned on two bulbs directly above them. All the while, she never let go of Allen's hand. She set her shoes next to her and grabbed Allen's left hand with both of her hands. She let her head lay on his shoulder.

Nyssa hadn't pictured this night turning out the way it was. She had thoughts of them eating together, talking a while, and then going home. Here they were, having a great night of laughter, drinks, and now holding hands. To any other grown up, this was a tame night, but to Nyssa, the simplicity of this date was what she loved most. The things others so take for granted was exactly what Nyssa needed. She wanted to be reminded that what made dating fun was beginning to show feelings and sharing basic moments of affection.

"This is going to be our spot. Let's make this a regular place for us to come to,"
Allen suggested as Nyssa turned to meet his eyes.

"I'm with that. That sounds wonderful, and if we are lucky, we can get that super nice waitress we had tonight. Let's not forget her," Nyssa said as her and Allen laughed.

"You are too silly, Nyssa. I love that about you. You can be so serious, but when you let your hair down and show your personality, you become so much more attractive to me."

"You don't even understand how silly I can truly be. You haven't seen anything yet."

"Oh okay, we will see. I wish we had more wine so I can see what you're talking about."

"Whatever, you couldn't handle more wine. I could tell you were walking all wobbly on the way over here. That was why I wanted to come over here, so you could sober up. Besides, if you would have stepped on my toes, it would have been me and you," Nyssa said, making a playful fist at Allen.

"Ha-ha, I don't think so. I was steady on my feet."

"Yeah steady as a one-legged chair."

"Now that was a good one!"

"You were as steady as someone riding a horse while taking a picture with a polaroid camera," Nyssa said, just going with the flow. She could tell that Allen was enjoying her silliness, so she was willing to oblige.

"Speaking of pictures. You want to know what I am thinking? I am thinking that we should have taken a picture back at that restaurant." What would be better for Allen than having a picture he could keep in his office.

"Oh, I got you." Nyssa reached into her small purse and pulled out her smart phone. "This phone has the best camera option of all the phones out there. Let's just take a picture with this," She said opening the camera app on her phone. Allen didn't care what kind of camera they were using, he just wanted the picture to be good so he could cherish it.

"Okay Allen, your dreams are about to come true. You get to hold me close, but I am watching you." Nyssa wiggled her way into Allen's lap. He let her sit in front of him so that her back was resting against his chest. Her perfume was intoxicating, and Allen relished it being on him.

"This is definitely a dream of mine, and I better take advantage of it before you change your mind. Besides, I didn't want to just grab you because you might have kicked my butt."

"You are right, because if I didn't want you to, I would have kicked your butt all over this beach," Nyssa said as she laughed and leaned back on Allen. As soon as Nyssa felt his body against hers, she immediately felt her heart skip a beat. She put the phone in her lap and grabbed Allen's arms, putting them around her in a hug. She was enjoying close human contact. She was feeling a sensation she hadn't felt in a long time. It was a sense of bonding and closeness she hadn't felt in years. Her isolation had her avoiding people and situations to appease her sadness. She fell victim to her pity, and it was sad to see now how far she had fallen.

Now, leaning back on Allen, she could once again smell his cologne. She took it in and closed her eyes. At this point, nothing was better. All the nights she cried, wondering if nights like this would ever happen again—if she would ever find anyone who would want to hold her again. It was putting her in another place, and she liked it. These past five months, Allen had been all she wanted and more. He was a calming voice and someone that could take her mind off her disease. She was sold on his personality. She found that to be very refreshing. She liked his honesty, and his demeanor was second to no one she had ever met. She was taken in by the level of respect he had for her. There were many qualities to him that she enjoyed, and for right now, he was her comfort.

For Allen, this was more than a dream come true. He was on cloud nine. He couldn't ask for a better moment than the one they were having. Who would have thought she would be inviting him to put his arms around her? He didn't want to ever let her go. This was the icing on his cake. This was more than he'd envisioned happening, so he was not going to rock the boat.

The mood was perfect for what was taking place in Nyssa's mind. Her mind was racing about all the things she wanted to do with her new outlook on life. She wanted to feel this way all the time, and she knew the only way that was going to happen was if she came out of her shell and lived her life.

Nyssa lifted her camera and made sure the flash was on. Even though the light bulbs above them were shining bright, she didn't want to take any chances on the picture being too dark. "Okay Allen, let's take this picture. I want you to smile, and you better smile like you mean it."

"Oh, don't worry, I will have a big cheesy smile on my face."

"Okay, here we go. One, two, three." Nyssa snapped a few pictures. In some, they were smiling; some they were being silly. The simple joy of taking pictures with someone you like brought a genuine smile to both their faces.

"Okay, make sure you send me those pictures. I want all of them," Allen said as he squeezed Nyssa tight.

Nyssa put her camera back in her purse and leaned

back onto Allen's chest. Allen rubbed his cheek against her cheek, causing her to almost melt at the touch. She reached up to caress the other side of his face. She hadn't done this in such a long time that she felt like she was in a dream. To finally touch her skin next to someone else's, and to feel the smoothness of his face next to hers, was moving her to tears. Only Nyssa knew how badly she had longed to be able to touch someone.

No one realized the desire she had to be caressed and loved. No one knew she was suffering on the inside— not just her body, but her spirit as well. It was so hard for Nyssa to face the world when all she wanted to do was hide from it. The pressure to be perfect, and in her case, to be disease free was truly disheartening. To be able to rub her face next to Allen's face may have seemed weird to some, but it was therapy for Nyssa, and she was going to take advantage of it. She didn't care that he was sweating; all she cared about was touching someone else.

Nyssa turned to look deeply into his eyes. He noticed her staring and smiled. Nyssa loved his smile, and she loved that she was the one who brought that smile to his face. Without breaking her gaze, and for reasons she didn't fully know, she began to move her lips closer to his. She did it without hesitation or a second thought. It was like two powerful magnets were pulling one to the other. It was slow and movie-like, but she was almost close enough to kiss him. Allen was welcoming the kiss as he began to move closer to Nyssa as well. As soon as their lips touched, a shiver went through her body. Nyssa didn't want to move, nor did she care if the earth stopped moving and reversed its spin. Nothing was going to pull her lips off Allen's lips.

The kiss was so soft and subtle, but Nyssa was more than happy. It was perfect.

Suddenly, a thought ran through her head. She began to get nervous as she realized that she had been so focused on her feelings, she'd forgotten a very important rule. Even though you can't pass HIV to someone by just holding their hand, giving them a hug, or kissing, Nyssa knew she had to tell people she did those things with—just in case they were afraid to do them with her. She knew it was only right to warn someone about her having the disease, especially if they were fearful of catching it. It was all about respecting other people, and Nyssa had just broken a big rule.

Now, her heart beat fast as she began to sweat. She pulled her lips away from his and looked at Allen anxiously. She looked at the innocence in his eyes and how they were so full of life. She wished she didn't have to tell him what she needed to. She wished there was a way to avoid it. She felt a connection with Allen, and she didn't want to lose that feeling. She also knew there was no way she could live with herself if she waited and he freaked out because she wasn't upfront with him. The embarrassment she faced in the restaurant the last time she was on a date almost drove her to suicide. If Allen did that to her, who was to say she wouldn't go through with it this time. If Allen couldn't overlook it, then who could? She couldn't deal with it if he acted like everyone else, because she felt like he was totally different.

As she looked him in the eye, she wanted to see how he would react without even telling him. She wanted to pretend like she'd just said it, and his reaction was, 'so what'. That was what she wanted to hear from Allen as she readied herself to drop this bomb on him.

"What's wrong?" Allen asked as he wiped sweat from her forehead. He began to feel like maybe he'd crossed a line in kissing her. Allen felt like all the signs were there, that she was okay with a kiss. Nyssa knew she had a worried look on her face. "Are you okay?" Allen asked Nyssa again, as she stared at him. Allen knew he would kick himself if he messed up a chance to be with Nyssa.

"I have something to tell you," Nyssa said as tears began to form in her eyes; she couldn't control them. She stood up, and immediately, Allen did the same. Things had gotten very awkward for them—and fast. She wanted to not tell him in the worst way. She wished she had something different to tell him—like, she wanted to see him more after tonight, or she thought the world of him. No, she had to tell him that she had a disease that could advance to the next stage any day now as it started a timer to the end of her life. She didn't want him to let her go. She wanted to hold his hand and above all, she wanted to feel human contact, for just a little while longer.

"What is it Nyssa?" Allen asked with a confused look on his face. His mind raced as he tried to play back the last few seconds in his mind to see where he went wrong. He grabbed her hands and held them. Nyssa wanted to continue to hold them, but she let his hands go. Allen didn't know what was going on, and the look on his face showed he felt responsible for whatever it was. The only thing he could tell was that she was in some sort of pain, and he didn't like the way it was affecting her. That made it even harder on Nyssa to tell him. The look of concern, and the way he made it seem like he cared so much, made her task even harder. Could she say what she had to say and run off Allen and be lonely all over again? She wanted to let the moment pass, but couldn't. They kissed, and the last thing she'd want would be for someone to do that to her—to deceive or keep from someone something as serious as announcing they have HIV when intimacy of any kind was involved. Even a simple kiss could make someone feel as if they were put in jeopardy of contracting HIV. As long as there was no blood transfer, then kissing a person with HIV was safe, but how would she know Allen was cool with that unless she said something. She had to say something because human decency demanded it. She needed to respect Allen, and if she cared about him, she would tell him. She was asking for honesty and truth, yet she stood there struggling with them both.

"Allen," Nyssa said as she paused to let a few tears roll down her face. All that mattered now was that Nyssa was bracing herself for what was coming next.

"Yes…" Allen said, watching her with confusion and angst. Allen couldn't understand what was taking place. He felt so horrible that he may have done something to cause her pain. They were having a wonderful time, and now it was time to rain on his parade.

"I have HIV."

3

Cederick Stewart

"So, you haven't talked to Allen?" Rachel asked. She heard Nyssa go quiet on the other end of the line.

"No."

"I can't believe he hasn't called you. He seemed to be so sweet and everything. As much as you bragged on him, I thought he would definitely be the one to understand you."

"Well, we will never know, because girl I played the fool last night and it carried over until this morning. After I told him about me having HIV, I didn't wait for his reply. I told him, grabbed my shoes, and made a b-line for my car. I turned my phone completely off, and as soon as I woke up this morning, I had my cell phone disconnected. That would be why we are talking on my home phone."

"Okay, and you did all that why?"

"I don't know Rachel."

Nyssa knew Rachel wasn't just asking her that question as a friend, but also as her doctor. Rachel knew all about Nyssa, and she knew her struggle, so she was trying to get some understanding as to why Nyssa would go to such extremes.

"Do I really want to face him again? What am I going to say?" Nyssa asked, getting emotional.

"What do you mean? You can say things like, 'Hi', or 'How are you?' You could even say, 'I had a wonderful time last night,'" Rachel said in a sarcastic way.

"You know what I mean. What can I say after I told him I have HIV? I can't pretend like everything is okay—not after saying something like that."

"Nyssa, this is what I am talking about. You are sitting up here feeling sorry for yourself. You know my rules, and I don't tolerate that. As your counselor and friend, I would advise you to stop acting like this and call Allen. He could be worried sick about you and wondering if you went over the deep end last night."

"Maybe he is, and I would love to think he cares that deeply for me, but I don't know if I can face him. What if he is glad that I went overboard and changed my number so he doesn't have to let me down by saying how he really feels?"

"I don't get it, Nyssa. Avoidance isn't always the answer. I am shaking my head at how you assume he is mad and doesn't like you at all, so let's just go to the furthest extreme and get rid of him. Okay that makes sense, let's cut off all ties to him, and your clients as well, unless you plan on sending them a notice of your new phone number. How much sense does that make Nyssa?"

"It makes none. I just don't want to get hurt anymore.

It felt so good talking to him because we had so much in common. He was so sweet, kind, and very respectful, and he treated me the way I want to be treated... and it felt nice. When we held hands, I felt a different touch than ever before. It was so amazing how the touch of his hand made me feel so good. I loved laying my head on his shoulder and touching his face next to mine. Those were simple things that I've missed so much. I loved every moment of last night. I don't truly know how he feels, but if that night is the only good thing that will come out of meeting Allen, then that is all I need. I don't want to ruin my thoughts of him by knowing how he truly feels about me since he knows I have HIV now."

"Nyssa, I can understand how you feel, but you must realize something. You know the paranoia is real when you deal with this disease. It is something you must take control of because it is the same paranoia that has kept you living the life of a hermit for three years. This jail sentence you have given yourself makes moments like last night seem so much worse than they truly are. You don't have any proof that Allen now looks at you negatively. You didn't stick around long enough to find out. You assumed the worst, ran off, and went as far left as possible by doing what you have done. We talk about this all the time—how people's fear of HIV comes from not knowing anything about it except the most harmful details. You are so knowledgeable when it comes to this disease—you've only been studying the virus since high school for goodness sake. If anyone can help ease someone's fear and anxiety about HIV, it's you. The only issue is, you are falling victim to the same thing you don't want other people falling victim to. You are so worried that people feel the way you would feel about finding out someone has HIV and didn't tell you." Rachel was making a great point.

Nyssa wiped the tears that rolled down her face. She didn't know what to do. She wanted to call Allen, but she was too afraid. She hadn't had any luck with anyone once she told them the truth. Every guy had run for the border— not one even pretended to care.

"Reality check is this Nyssa... how long are you going to let this disease dictate your life? You have HIV, we get that, but does it have to be the end-all-be-all? You know exactly what to do to control this disease, and you have been doing that and beyond. You are taking your medicine, and you have been blessed to not have any side effects at all. You may feel like God allowed this to happen, and you are not happy about it, but I also know that you have been blessed with this treatment regimen you are on. You are the only test subject that has had no side effects, and the medicine is doing everything we thought it could. Your T-cell count is rising and that is always a wonderful sign that all things are working in your favor. Remember, you are blessed regardless if you think so or not. It is not up to how you feel that decides if God is working things out in your favor. What we do know is that, if you keep on living like this, you will get depressed, then you will be in a funk that no one and nothing can bring you out of. When you start feeling like God isn't there, and has left you alone, you will leave room for the enemy to tear you apart." As Nyssa listened to Rachel, she felt like throwing the phone across the room.

She wondered why Rachel didn't feel sorry for her. This was her doctor, and her best friend, but she seemed to be a robot when it came to dealing with Nyssa and her

HIV. In Nyssa's eyes, Rachel was showing no compassion or concern for how she truly felt. Rachel must have forgotten that Nyssa was a victim and nothing else. This wasn't something she deserved or something she earned by living a life that lead to HIV.

"The enemy is tearing me apart on the inside. Every day, I live with an enemy looking for a weak spot or an off day, so it can turn the tide and take control of me. An enemy waiting on me to let my guard down so it can do what it is here to do and I live with that reality every day and it isn't easy at all."

"I understand that, and that's why I have been on the phone with you these past three hours, trying to remind you that you have a reason to live and a reason to keep on fighting. Nyssa, you have been such a blessing to every client you have. Every survey on you brags about how you are just a Godsend to them. Your compassion and dedication means the world to them. Your clients are fighting to live every day. They face the same enemy you face, but they are at the point where they are learning to understand who their enemy is, and they refuse to let it win. You on the other hand, know your enemy like the back of your hand, yet you are not even trying to put up a fight. Who does that? Who would let an enemy win when they have all the tools to defeat it?"

Nyssa listened closely to what Rachel was saying, and deep down inside, she knew Rachel was right. Nyssa had no fight in her. She wasn't doing anything productive to help herself overcome the disease other than taking her medications. She left the fight up to the medicine and hoped for the best. By putting all the responsibility on the pills, failure would ride on their shoulders, and she would be blameless.

"You're right, Rachel. I want to fight, but I also want to feel sorry for myself. I am not going to lie. I want the attention that comes with being a victim. That's why it has been so easy for me to do what I have been doing these past three years. To have people check up on me, and worry about how I am doing is what gets me through my day. That constant reminder that you are on someone's mind, and they care enough to call you, is what I crave," Nyssa confessed in a moment of blunt honesty.

"Thank you for finally being truthful with me on this. I could tell that was how you were feeling, and that is why I have been so hard on you. You preach it to your clients, but you don't hold yourself to those same standards. You tell them how helpful honesty is, and if they truly want to be helped, they would say exactly how they feel. I have to beg you and make you feel bad before you open to me. You see how the enemy works by constantly causing separation and isolation."

"I know, I shouldn't have let this enemy do this. I wasn't even trying to do anything about it. I sat up here day-by-day, wasting away and letting precious time go by as I was too fearful to even mention this enemy out loud."

"Are we talking about the same enemy?"

"What do you mean? We are talking about HIV," Nyssa said taken aback by Rachel's question.

"No Sweetie, we are talking about Satan. That is the enemy you are losing to. He is whipping your head, and you are letting him do it to you daily. He is stealing all your joy and your desire to enjoy this life that God has given you. I have sat back too long babying you and allowing you to have this pity-party. The truth of the matter is this, regardless if you have a pity-party or a blessed life party,

God is still in control of the outcome, and you must live your life as if you are going to win. If you live your life like you are already defeated, then you will waste the years you have left, and you will look back and wish you had made the most of your life like God was expecting you to. If you waste this opportunity, then you must live with it for the rest of your life. So, let's pray about this now, because I have to go."

"Okay, let's pray." As the prayer was being said, Nyssa sat on the line crying her eyes out. She knew it was time to toughen up and fight. She had taken too many blows these past three years, and now it was time to do what she needed to do. Quietly, she thanked God for Rachel, because there was no telling where Nyssa would be without her. Being there for her like the sister she didn't have, Rachel had done so much that Nyssa could never repay her for. This fight was going to be for Rachel as well. This prayer was needed, and when Rachel was done praying, Nyssa felt rejuvenated and ready to change.

"Alright Nyssa, I love you girl. Be strong and I will talk to you later."

"I love you too. Thanks for everything Rachel. Bye." Nyssa hung up the phone. She just sat there crying for a while longer. She cried because she had been here before and hated this feeling. She hated the aftermath of telling someone she had HIV. She hated the waiting to see if they would call her. She hated to think about running into that person in a public place and being treated like an outcast. There was so much to worry about and nothing to feel good about. Having HIV was the hardest thing she could imagine having. People, who know a lot about the disease, take the simple precautions necessary to guard against it, and people who don't know take major precautions. Regardless, the fact remains that avoidance is what they all choose.

Nyssa felt that she could deal with the fact that people wouldn't want physical contact with her, even if they still talked to her. She wasn't asking people to sleep with her. All she wanted was to be treated like any other normal, healthy person. It was as if she lived in a bubble, and no one could touch her; she hated that feeling. She wanted to be comforted and caressed. She wanted someone to touch her in a way that said, 'I don't care what you have, I am going to touch you anyway.' She wanted someone to just hold her hand, but not just any kind of way—the way Allen had.

She'd never had a feeling like that before. It was the subtlest thing to do, but it felt so different. It felt soothing and made her feel safe. That safety and comfort was what she desired right now. To have him sitting next to her right now and telling her, 'Don't worry, I am not going anywhere' was what she wanted to hear Allen say more than anything else. To be reassured that no disease, or anything else, was going to stop them from being together. But, she quickly dispelled that last thought. She knew better than to get her hopes up, feeling like there was even a small chance they could be together. The pain that came from rejection and the despair of anticipation was too much for her to handle. She had experienced those times when guys would make a scene and call her out, belittling her for having HIV, but sometimes the worst rejection was silence—where guys ended conversations on the phone or finished a date, but were very standoffish. Then never called back—not the next day, not the next week, not the next month, or the next year. Nope, no communication at all. Just a silent rejection that felt like she had never met them at all. Almost as if their paths never crossed, and that hurt Nyssa worst because she was always so good to each guy she dated. She went above and beyond to make them feel special. She wanted it to be hard for them to leave when they found out about her disease. Truth of the matter, it was the exact opposite. It was too easy for them to leave and too hard on her to watch them all go. Nyssa wasn't conceited, but confident in the fact that she was a very beautiful woman. If she was 100% healthy, she would have to turn guys away. But, now the shoe was on the other foot and she didn't reach their standards.

She couldn't blame those men for how they felt, and she knew it wasn't right to even be mad at them. It wasn't their fault she had HIV, and it was not totally their fault that they were afraid of it. In a way, it was totally smart to be fearful of getting HIV because there was no turning back from it. Nyssa just laid in her bed as she stared at the ceiling. She so wanted to just float right up to the ceiling, then through it, and off in the atmosphere. Then, she wouldn't have to worry about anyone or anything as she drifted off and became part of the universe.

Nyssa closed her eyes. She was so tired. Sleep was hard to come by last night. After she drove home like a madman, she sat in the shower for over an hour crying. She tried to soak away her tears, then gathered the strength to crawl into her bed. She cried the whole night. So now, she was going to try to rest and think about nothing else. Nyssa grabbed her favorite comforter, rolled up tight like a burrito, and went to sleep.

Allen walked the familiar path that took him to

Nathan's headstone. The same oak tree that had been there since the first time he came looked as big and strong as ever. As he got closer, he could still see the words carved into the tree. Five years ago, there was this little boy with his mother, and they were visiting a headstone nearest the tree. Allen could hear the little boy say that the tree was God watching over his dad. The little boy had carved the words, 'Thank you God', into the tree. It was still visible as ever in the day time.

As soon as he turned onto the sidewalk that leads directly to Nathan's spot, he was hit by a wave of emotions. Memories came flooding back, and he fought back tears. He made it to Nathan's headstone and noticed the fresh flowers that were probably brought out by Nathan's mom. He walked up to the headstone and he fist-bumped Nathan's name as a sign of their friendship. He then sat next to the headstone and just stared off into the distance. There was so much on his mind, and he wished he had Nathan here to bounce things off. The way Nathan always gave a different perspective on things helped Allen understand his situation better.

"Nathan, what's up man? Sorry about not being able to come yesterday. I had a jam-packed day." To Allen, that felt like a lie even though it was true. "I did talk to your mom, though, and it was good hearing her voice. I need to be better about not just calling once a year, but to check up on her more often. She told me she was going to visit you, but I knew I couldn't come with her like I have in the past. I am sure it was good for her to visit on her own and say things she probably wouldn't say around me." Allen knew that went for him as well. He would just say the surface-level things that were going on in his life and make small talk with Nathan's mom. Nothing like what he would say if she wasn't with him.

"I know you will be glad to hear that the coffee shop is doing very well. I am doing it in a major way, and I have been praying to God about possibly opening another location, so I can 'maximize my efforts'—like you always said you would do with your steak restaurant. Yep, doing all I can to make all I can. This is the first year I can tell you I have zero worries when it comes to my coffee shop. I have capital now, a great staff, and the best location around town. This is how I expected it to be, but I am so blessed that God has let my dreams come true." Allen knew God had blessed him. He'd ended up with a prime spot next to the museum, and with no credit, experience, or references to back his dream. The bank chose him over three other owners that had been in the game for years. They basically overlooked what was important on the application to give him a chance, and for that Allen felt it was God's hand in control.

"Nathan, since the last time I visited you a few things have changed. Well, for one, I met a woman five months ago, and man oh man is she fine. She is a doctor and so beautiful. She is by far the finest woman around, and if you were here, I would have to keep you away from her. You my boy and all, but I would fight you to the death for her. She is everything I want in a woman and more. Ever since I first met her, I have been head over heels for her. We went on our first date last night. Your boy was too scared to ask her out before last night, but I finally did it. We went to that one spot on the beach where they play music. It was such a wonderful night until the end. I had no clue it would turn out the way it did. We were having a very quiet moment and everything was perfect. We were talking, laughing, and getting along and it was awesome. I moved in for a kiss, and it was perfect.

It couldn't have been a better moment, but then she dropped some news on me. She told me she has HIV. Yep, that is right, I said HIV. I know what you are thinking, and I thought the same thing. Before I could reply, she took off. I don't know if she was a track star or not, but she was in the wind. I tried to keep up, but you know I wasn't any good at sports at all. She dusted me. I looked all over the parking lot for her, but all I heard was screeching tires. Just like that, what I thought was a beginning turned out to be an end. I had such high hopes for us.

I made all kinds of plans in my mind. I had already seen us engaged. I was going to do something romantic and go all out to make her feel special. Next, the wedding was going to be second to none. I can see her now walking down the aisle in her wedding dress, looking like a campfire in the snow. I know I would be praying that she wouldn't change her mind and run off like a runaway bride. After last night, I am not so sure it wouldn't have happened. I bet you, dress-in-all; she would have still been fast. Ha-ha, I am still tripping over that. At that precise moment, society would have expected me to run, not her. I mean, she kissed me, and it felt like she didn't hold anything back. She was into it, and so was I. Wasn't that cause enough to run after her. Like I said, what I thought was a beginning, is now the end."

As soon as the credits began to roll on her movie,

her home phone rang. Nyssa rolled over and looked at the caller ID. She smirked because it was her father, and he always seemed to call after something happened to her.

"Hello," Nyssa said, pretending she didn't know it was him.

"Hey, baby. I was returning your call. You left me a message that had me disturbed. Now what exactly is going on over there?"

"Sorry to alarm you, Dad. I seriously overreacted last night."

"Oh, how so?"

"Well, I was on a date with a guy. Everything was going fine, and we were hugging on the beach. I had a little too much to drink, and I got caught up in the moment. We got close and I kissed him."

"You did? Did he know you have HIV?" Her father said with concern in his voice.

"No Dad, he didn't." Nyssa couldn't hide the disappointment in her voice and it was directed at herself.

"Nyssa, come on. You promised me you wouldn't do that."

"It was a slip up Dad. I liked this guy, and he told me he liked me. We were drinking, but that is still no excuse. I promise you, it won't happen again."

"We had the talk Nyssa, and you said you understood how serious this is. Somebody will hurt you if you do that to the wrong person, and I couldn't live with that. So, what happened after you kissed him? Did you tell him then?"

"I told him immediately after it happened."

"What did he say?"

"Well, we were in the middle of an intimate moment. We had taken a walk along the beach and stopped to rest along the wall. We were hugging and that's when it happened. When I told him, I ran off and drove straight home. Basically, I don't know how he feels. I didn't even give him the chance to say anything."

"So, let me get this straight. You told him, and then just ran off? You don't have any clue how he truly feels? What was the look on his face when you told him?"

"I am not sure. I don't think it was a look of shock. It's hard for me to remember because I was so teary eyed. I didn't want to tell him, but I knew it was only right."

"Good Nyssa, you did the right thing. You realized your mistake, and you immediately tried to rectify it. I am not quite sure if running off was the best thing to do, but if I recall correctly, you were pretty fast in track, so I'm sure you kicked up a little dust," Nyssa's dad said, trying to make light of the situation. Nyssa smiled.

"I wish I could tell you that it was a graceful exit, but it wasn't. I almost lost my balance a couple of times because of the sand. I didn't fall, but still, it wasn't my greatest moment. Let's just say, no one was impressed with the way I left," Nyssa said, trying to find humor in her actions.

"You are still silly as always. I have always loved that about you. It is times like these that you remind me of your mother."

"Oh, no you didn't. I hope I never remind you of Cathy," Nyssa said defensively. Ever since her mom left when she was little, Nyssa stopped calling her 'mom', and started calling her by her first name. To Nyssa, her mother had never earned the title of 'mom', even though God gave it to her. No loving mother would ever abandon her family or be that selfish. She didn't even try to make their family work, but instead ran and hid from the responsibility. There was nothing she hated more than to be told that she and Cathy had anything in common.

"Nyssa, that is still your mother, like it or not. I am not too happy that I married her, but I still tell people she was my wife—even though technically she never was. She checked out early in the marriage, and when she got pregnant, everything spiraled downhill from there. The conversations we had while we dated were centered on raising a family. I don't recall any red flags or anything that would have given me a clue that she would bolt like that."

"Exactly, and that is why I want no part of any comparison to her. She is a quitter, and she runs and hides from her battles."

As soon as Nyssa said that, her heart was convicted. Everything she had just said applied to her exactly. She never thought about it like that before. She knew she didn't like anything about her mother, but the similarities were there. Not only was Nyssa a carbon copy of her mother in looks, but also in actions, and Nyssa hated that the most. When she was growing up, it was always the comments of, 'she is beautiful like her mother' or 'she runs like her mother'. That always took the joy out of her. That was why she didn't run track in college, because she just so happened to attend the same college her mother had. A few track records she could have easily broken were held by her mother. But, she didn't want any more comparisons, and she didn't want to be known as 'Cathy's daughter'.

"Nyssa, you are dealing with so much with this disease, and I know it is not easy. It has consumed your whole life and I mean every aspect of it. I know you hate to hear this, but even though your mother's fight is not the same, it is similar. She ran from her fight. She gave up and gave in to the easy way. She didn't use what God gave her to fight her battle. Nope, she threw in the towel and ran. She had a husband, a child, and a family that would have encouraged and loved her every day. She wasn't facing her fears alone. She had us, and we would have done everything in our power to help her, but she couldn't see that. She only focused on her issue. That is so like what you are doing now. You are only focused on the fact that you have HIV, and not the fact that you know exactly how to live a rich, full life with the disease—and with no problem, I might add. Don't think for a second that God didn't give you a fight that you can easily win. Many people fight battles with things they have no clue on how to defeat, but you were given an advantage on your enemy.

Ever since high school, you have become well-versed in what makes your enemy tick. You know the ins-and-outs of how it thrives, yet you have not used one of its weaknesses against it. You have people living twenty plus years with HIV, and yet you feel like you have a death sentence and won't be afforded what they have. God wants to use you, but you are so focused on the disease, that you can't even see anything else." Nyssa's father was making all the sense in the world. Nyssa just sat on the phone and listened. Her father was always the one seeing things the way she should see them. He was always on time with his wisdom and always gave credit to God for his perfect timing.

"You are so right Dad. I have been running and not putting up a fight, and that is so like Cathy. I don't want any of her characteristics, but if I had to pick one, it wouldn't be running from responsibilities. I am glad you explained it like you did. I see now that God has prepared me for this fight, and I couldn't see that because I was just focusing on who the fight was with. I know HIV has a winning record, and that has scared me the most. All this time, I thought I was afraid to die, when I was acting like I was afraid to live. Afraid to live a life that I have been given. I pretended like I was already dead. You are totally right. I know this enemy, and I will kick its butt."

"Yes, you have all the game tape on your enemy. You have years of breakthroughs to help you fight this fight. Baby, don't let this thing take your will to live away."

"It's not going to Dad. I won't waste my life over something like this."

"Nyssa, don't let it take your life away by having you not living it to its fullest. You are thirty-four years old, and if God says so, you have plenty more years to experience all God wants you to experience in this world. This disease has zapped your desire to be a part of God's plan for your life. Your whole focus is based upon this disease, and guess what, there are people living with AIDS out there trying to enjoy each day as if it is their last. You are as healthy as they come, minus the HIV, and yet you act like you are on your deathbed. This disease has tricked you, and so has Satan. You are letting him use your disease to isolate you from those that love you and God. Then, he will be able to torment you and cause you to not see the good in your situation. HIV is not ideal for anyone, but I believe that you can overcome this. It is going to take you believing that."

"You know what Dad? I thank God for you and Rachel, because both of you have given me the fuel I need to start living my life and stop feeling sorry for myself. I will be better, and I hope I can make you proud as I become more like you and less like Cathy."

"You know you will not be happy until you forgive

her, right?"

"I know Dad, and who knows what the future holds for us."

"Okay, so you are better now? I hope so, because I am missing all my college football talking to you."

"Whatever. I love you so much Dad. Until we see each other again."

"Love you more baby. Bye."

Nyssa hung up the phone and wiped the tears off her face. Today had been a day of self-evaluation and coming up with a plan to make the most of her situation. She knew she had so much to do, and she needed to find a way to get the courage to talk to Allen again.

4

Nyssa walked into Allen's coffee shop after circling the parking lot for twenty minutes. The anxiety from not knowing what to expect was playing major tricks on her mind. She walked in and looked for the table she had the very first time she was in the coffee shop and found it unoccupied. Her plan was to make a b-line right to the table and try her best to blend in until she could talk to Allen. Nyssa didn't want to look towards the area where the coffee was prepared because that was where Allen normally worked, especially if it was crowded. He was a master when it came to preparing coffee under pressure.

The coffee shop wasn't too crowded, but it was busy enough to where he would feel the need to help. Nyssa tried to have tunnel vision as she walked in, but it was not working. As soon as the door swung open, her gaze went right to the coffee counter. She scanned the area, but didn't see Allen. That was perfectly fine with her because she wasn't ready to speak to him that soon. She wanted the comfort of the seat at her table to give her the support she needed now. She tried to walk straight to the table without speaking to anyone, but it was short lived as one of her favorite workers spotted her.

"Hey Nyssa, what a surprise seeing you. Are you meeting one of your clients tonight?" Emily asked as she stopped wiping tables to walk over. One thing Nyssa loved about Emily was her bubbly personality; it made it truly hard to not like her. She always had a big smile on her freckled baby face, and her red ponytail made her look younger than she was. Allen was always bragging about how wonderful she was to have at the coffee shop. Even when they were swamped and overwhelmed, Emily was always encouraging them to keep up the good work.

"Hi Emily, no I am not meeting a client tonight. I just came in for a cup of coffee. I was in the neighborhood and thought I would make sure you guys are working as hard as Allen says you do."

"We have been overwhelmed today. We just slowed down about an hour ago. I am talking about nonstop customers."

"Well that's a good thing."

"It was, but we introduced a new coffee today, and it complicated things as we tried to get familiar with making it."

"Really, was it a hit?"

"Oh, you should try it. It is a vanilla, toffee, and marshmallow blend. It sounds like it is going to be real sweet, but surprisingly, it isn't. The customers went crazy for it. It is so good cold or hot."

"Sounds good, I think I will have a cup hot."

"Okay, I will let them know, just have a seat. I will also let Allen know you are here, but I will warn you, he hasn't been himself today. He wasn't as happy as he normally is. We're all kind of worried about him." Nyssa didn't know how to feel about what she'd just heard. Maybe he was sad because he really liked her when he thought she didn't have HIV. But, now that he knew the truth, he was trying to find a way to let her go.

"Oh, I hate to hear that," Nyssa said trying to sound surprised.

"Well, I'm just glad it wasn't because of you he's sad. I thought maybe you guys broke up or something. You didn't come by today to get your coffee, so I didn't want to assume the worst. I know he cares about you, as he always talks about you when you come to get your coffee, and he gushes about you all day long. When you didn't come by this morning, his whole demeanor was so different. Seeing you now makes me feel like maybe you came by to cheer him up."

"Well, I hope I can cheer him up. I was so busy all day that I didn't have time to stop by this morning."

"Oh, you must have had an emergency with one of your clients because usually nothing stops you from coming by to get your coffee."

"You could say that. It took a while to get my client to see things the way they really are," Nyssa said, knowing good and well that she was the client who had an emergency. So technically, she wasn't lying to Emily.

"You are so awesome to me. The way you take care of your clients and show such a loving touch. Allen tells us how you are always going above and beyond for your clients, and that is so special. Most doctors treat patients as clients and not friends, but I can tell you care about them.

You must be such a blessing to them," Emily said as she showed her winning smile. Nyssa was touched by her words and knew that, when it came to her clients, it was all about them and going out of her way to ensure they were taken care of to the best of her ability.

"I try Emily. I want them to know I care and that I understand what they are going through."

"I am sure you do an excellent job of that, and I hope you can do the same job on Allen because he really needs it. I hate to see him like this." Emily's smile morphed into a look of concern.

"Me too. Do me a favor Emily, don't interrupt him just yet."

"Okay, no problem. Let me go and get your coffee."

Nyssa walked over to her table and sat down so she could face the counter. If Allen walked out behind the counter, he would have a full view of her. She wanted to see what the look on his face would be when he saw her. Nyssa was no longer going to hide and cower behind her disease. She was going to face whatever situation it brought head on and deal with the consequences courageously. Nyssa watched Emily make her coffee and thanked her when she brought it over. Nyssa took a sip. It was better than Emily said it would be! It had an ever-so-slightly sweet taste that complimented the strong flavor of the coffee. Nyssa knew she would order this coffee on a regular basis.

As she sat at the table, she knew she needed a few more minutes to gather the courage to face Allen. However, she also knew it was about ten minutes until closing, and he would begin his usual closing routine soon. Nyssa's intentions were to write a letter, drop it off to whoever was working, and slip off quietly into the night. The whole drive to the shop, something in her spirit told her not to drop the letter off, but to have a face-to-face. Nyssa was going to trust her gut; even though it had failed her every other time she felt she was doing the right thing.

Every one of those situations turned out terrible for her, and what made this time worse was that she had physical contact with someone before telling them. All the other times, she was on the second or third date, and every date was filled with talking, but no touching. Her date with Allen was so different because they had been talking for months, and she had grown fond of him. She wanted to have a relationship with him. Their kiss crossed the line in so many ways, and that scared her the most.

Maybe he thinks he has HIV because of the peck on the lips we shared? Maybe he is plotting on ways to get back at me, like spreading the word that I have HIV? She had to fight the urge to continue thinking negatively because that was the old Nyssa. The new Nyssa was going to go with a different approach. She was going to approach with an open mind and react once she knew how people felt about her, and not what she assumed they were feeling. Nyssa began to look at the pictures hanging on the wall of the coffee shop. They were all so detailed and beautiful—the way the focal point of each picture was in color and the background was black and white. Nyssa hadn't seen that technique before, so she leaned in closer to the picture nearest to her to see who the photographer was.

"Majestically Captured," Nyssa read the engraving out loud. She noticed that the gallery was in Las Vegas. She was going to look them up because she wanted to know more about them. If all their pictures were as good as this, then Nyssa knew she wanted some for her home and office. Here was a black and white picture of a cup of coffee with steam coming out of it. The cup was sky-blue and the background was an empty coffee shop in black and white. The cup stood out so beautifully. You could see the steam rising from the cup, and it was white, but it had a hint of the sky-blue as well. From a distance, it looked like the picture was in 3D, but up close you could see it wasn't. Nyssa knew it was a wonderful concept, and she wanted to see if there was a specific style that might be perfect for her office and home.

"I personally picked that picture myself. I visited Las Vegas and was told that there was a gallery I needed to check out. I heard that the concepts there were second to none and, if I wanted to have some art that was next level that was the place to be. So, I went there and was blown away by the style and technique of the pictures there. The owner, Majestic is her name, she gave me a tour, and I knew I needed some of her work in my shop," Allen said as he stood next to the table looking at the picture. Nyssa looked up, and her heart almost came out of her chest. He totally surprised her. She wanted to make sure she saw him first, because she wanted to see the look on his face when he first realized she was there. That would've told her so much about where she stood with him.

"May I sit with you?" Allen asked as he smiled at her.

"Yes, you may." Nyssa was feeling shy for the first time in forever. It was a very uncomfortable and awkward feeling that she couldn't explain, but it was weighing on her. At least on the phone, she would have been in her comfort zone and in the sanctuary of her loft.

Allen sat down and looked across the table at Nyssa. She didn't want to make eye contact with him, but needed to see what his eyes would tell her—compassion or rejection.

"I see you tried our new coffee. So, what do you think? Is it too sweet?" Allen asked as he glanced down at Nyssa's coffee cup.

"I like it a lot. I was very impressed," Nyssa replied, trying to read his mood. Was this the calm before the storm?

"Okay, Mr. Allen, we are leaving. Everything is shut down and cleaned. See you in the morning. Bye Nyssa," Emily said as she walked towards the door with the other co-workers.

"Excuse me, Nyssa," Allen said as he got up to give them all a hug and lock the door behind them. He put up the closed sign, and pulled down the shades in all the windows. Nyssa watched his body language closely. It was the same thing she did with her clients. She was taught in college that working with clients with such serious illnesses required her to look for certain behaviors. She couldn't be too carefree and let her guard down, because anyone dealing with a deadly illness could snap without warning. It didn't happen all the time, but Nyssa knew she should be on guard. What if he asked them to leave so he could go off on her for possibly putting his life at risk? What if he put his hands on her? Nyssa hated when her paranoia took over her mind and made her always think the worst. She didn't honestly think Allen would do anything to harm her. Of all people, he was the last person she would think that of.

So, she started to refocus her thoughts as Allen made himself a cup of coffee. As he was walking back to the table, she braced herself. After all, she had already gone through the embarrassment in public numerous times, so a one-on-one humiliation wasn't going to be that bad. Allen sat down and stared at his cup. Nyssa didn't like the dead silence, but she didn't know if it was best for him to speak first, or her. In all fairness, it was her issue that was the cause of all this drama, so Nyssa knew she needed to gain the courage to say something. Allen took a sip of his coffee, but he kept staring into his cup as if to say, 'you need to explain yourself.'

"Okay, Allen. Can you look at me?" Nyssa asked as she stared intently at Allen's face. If she was going to do this, she was going to look him dead in his eyes, and face the music. Allen looked up and tried to muster a smile, but in Nyssa's eyes, it looked very forced.

"I really don't know where to start or how to start," Nyssa began as she fought back tears. She wished she didn't have to ever have this conversation again. "I want you to know that there is no way I would ever, ever, ever purposely try to hurt you in any way. I hope you know that I am not that type of person. I felt so bad about what took place the other night. I let myself get caught up in the moment. You don't know how special that night was for me. I couldn't believe I was finally out enjoying myself, and it was even more special because it was with you. I hadn't truly been out in years and that night made me feel so normal. It reminded me of times before my sickness. I couldn't ruin that moment because I needed it down in my spirit more than anything else, so I didn't have the heart to tell you that I have HIV. Not that night, no way was I going to take that night and trash it up by revealing the mood killer.

See, that was why with all prior conversations, I would avoid certain questions or changed the subject, because I was trying to avoid revealing it. I wanted to go out with you on so many occasions, but having HIV put a paralyzing fear in me that wouldn't go away. I wish I didn't have it, and with every fiber in my being, I have tried to pray it away." Nyssa's eyes let go of the tears that had welled up. This soul-sharing issue was hard to fathom and even harder to talk about. Nyssa could only imagine how it felt to be on the other side of this conversation. What would be going through her mind? It was not like a client telling her this because this was way more personal. This was someone she had strong feelings for and it was hard to think about.

"I feel terrible, and I am truly sorry. It's just that, I really like you, and I know I was selfish for not telling you about my situation. How could I be so selfish on one hand and claim to really care about you on the other hand? It's almost like I lose if I tell you or I lose if I don't. I have never felt as comfortable with someone as I am with you. I have prayed to God for someone that will love me despite HIV, and I prayed that someone was you. But, I was too scared to truly find out if that was true, so I kept it to myself. I would rather pretend you were the one, than to have the courage to find out for sure. At least when I pretend you already know.

At the end of the day, I should have been truthful and not selfish. So, will you please forgive me for not being open and honest about me having HIV?" Nyssa asked. She really didn't know what else to say because she'd laid it out as plain as she could. Now, it was time to brace herself for whichever side of the fence Allen was on. She knew the side she wanted him to be on, but it was up to him. Allen sipped on his coffee, then put his cup down and looked up at Nyssa. Nyssa's heart was pounding. She thought she might throw up. She didn't want to prolong the silence while he got his thoughts together. She only wanted him to get straight to the point about how he felt; that would be easier to accept than a long dialogue that would only delay the inevitable.

"I knew all along," Allen said as he took a deep breath.

"What?"

"Yeah, I knew already."

"You knew? How?" Nyssa asked, shocked. She immediately began to play back as many conversations in her mind as possible to figure out where she'd slipped up.

"Well, I googled you a long time ago. I wanted to know all I could about you when we first met, and the deeper I searched, the more I found. One day, I found this article after you won an award, and in the article, it said that not only were you one of the best HIV doctors in the United States, but you were also the only one that had HIV."

Nyssa could not believe what Allen had just told her, but she also couldn't believe how naïve she was about the internet. It never dawned on her that somewhere in cyberspace there was information about her having HIV.

"How long have you known?" Nyssa asked, still trying to come to grips with this revelation.

"I have known about three months now."

"Three months? Why you never said anything?"

"That was something I needed you to tell me. How would I just come out and ask you that? For one, I didn't want you to know I was looking you up online," Allen said as he began to smile. That single smile was successful in getting Nyssa's nerves to start to calm down. "You really can't be too sure of anyone these days, and I was just looking out for myself."

"Honestly, I am not mad that you would look me up online, because I did the same to you. But, here I am embarrassed, because I was thinking that I was keeping a secret from you, and you knew already. I mean, you have known for three months and never said a word."

"Nyssa, when I found out, I was shocked. I never thought in a million years you would have HIV. I just thought you were a workaholic that didn't have time for dating or just extremely picky. I couldn't believe you were single, but I was thankful you were. Was it a little hard to soak in at first? Yes, it was. Was it ever a deal breaker? No."

Nyssa's heart skipped a beat.

"I wish that wasn't part of the package for you. I wish it was something simpler and not so complex. I wish I could live with anything other than HIV."

"I bet you do, but you have done a good job working with the hand you have been dealt. You are alive, looking very healthy, and are drop dead gorgeous," Allen said putting Nyssa at ease. Every positive compliment reinforced the truth in his words. Nyssa never imagin

"Thank you, but having HIV is so hard because I worry a lot, I am sad a lot, and I am mad at God a lot. I want to be normal so badly it hurts. I can tell you that talking to you on the phone daily made me feel normal. It felt like I was in a relationship with someone who loved me for who I am. Now that I know you know, I don't know what to do because the ball is in your court. I want you to know that I really like you and would love for things to stay the same, but if you choose to pull away and go your separate way, I truly understand. All I ask is that you pull away slowly and not abruptly. That is my only request, but it is fully your choice because it is your life," Nyssa said as she finished her coffee and sat back in her chair, awaiting Allen's decision.

"Nyssa, I want you to know that I care for you very deeply. Ever since our first real conversation, I knew that I would fall for you. Just how deep and well-versed you were on everything we talked about made me feel that I could talk to you forever. We never had any dull conversations, and when you are truly being you, by acting silly, I was hooked. I love everything about you. I love the sound of your voice, and how it soothes me when you are serious, and how your laugh always brings a smile to my face. I love how you stick to a schedule, and at times, are very predictable. How you go above and beyond for your clients to the point where you give all for them until you have nothing left for you. I am overwhelmed by your beauty and how it makes my heart jump when I see you. Your smile is worth the wait, and I love the way you look at me when you come to the coffee shop. You are everything I could possibly want in a woman."

"But?" Nyssa asked as she prepared for what came next.

"But, I want you to know that I am not going anywhere."

"What? For real? What about me having HIV? That doesn't scare you?" Nyssa asked as her heart beat faster and faster.

"Nope. Remember I have known for three months and it didn't stop me from calling you and pursuing you. I feel in my heart that I am supposed to be with you. As I think about how all the things played out over the past nine years, I see that God was maturing and growing me for what was to come."

"I hope so Allen, but I am still a little scared. No one I have met so far has been willing to be with me, but you are choosing to. It scares me because I don't want you to change your mind after reading up on HIV, and what could happen if you get it."

"That is not going to happen. I already know a lot

about HIV. My best friend Nathan died from AIDS nine years ago."

"Oh, I hate to hear that."

"Me too. I took it hard. He got AIDS from having unprotected intercourse. All our friends shunned him, and at the end of his life, it was only me and his family left in his corner. I hated that. I loved him like a brother, and it hurt me to see him waste away from what AIDS did to him. Now I understand why I had a strong desire to know all I could about AIDS when I found out he had it. How I would still hug him and touch him because I knew that I was safe. I now see that God was preparing me for you."

Nyssa's eyes began to tear up again. That was the best thing she had ever heard from a man; words she didn't think she would ever hear. All the rejection, embarrassment, and loneliness she had endured by other men had her thinking HIV sapped all that was good about her. The pain from having men act like she was the lowest of the low didn't help her self-esteem at all. Now, Allen was telling her that he didn't care if she had HIV; he was willing to be with her, and it was so clear that God was still with her. All those days she complained to God that no one would want her. How she cried to him because three letters meant that she was going to go through the rest of her life alone. Nyssa resigned herself to a life of loneliness, but now she knew that God had the final say on her life, and she was beginning to understand that more.

"Allen, I want to be perfectly honest with you from this moment on. If you are not going anywhere, and you already know I have HIV, I would like to tell you how I got it because I want to remove any fears you have of me being promiscuous or careless with my life."

"If you are okay with telling me right now because I

know it must be hard to tell people."

"It is, but I am at the point to where I know it is a part of who I am. How can I avoid the conversation on it? There are so many circumstances where it is extremely important that someone I am with knows. I am not talking about dating, but if I am at the mall, in a car, in someone's home etc. If an accident happens, and I am cut or bleeding, I need for them to know that I have HIV so they don't have any contact with my blood. That sounds so harsh every time I say it, but it is the truth of the matter. I must be extremely cautious, always. I would hate for someone's life to be drastically changed because I didn't inform them. That was why I was so mad at myself, because I should have told you sooner. I just didn't want to run you off but here is my story.

So, I was doing an outreach project that I started at the hospital I work at. We have been going to Swaziland, Africa for many years to administer HIV trial drugs to the people there. Well, the last time I was there, I was in a car accident on my way back to the airport. I was taken to a Swaziland hospital, and it was there that I was given a blood transfusion with tainted blood. That's how I contracted the virus." Nyssa could feel herself getting emotional. It was so hard to tell that story without feeling sad because it reminded her of such a tragic accident.

Allen got out of his chair and pulled it closer to Nyssa. He sat down and grabbed her hand, gently caressing it with a soft touch. As soon as he did, the flood gates opened for Nyssa's emotions. It made her feel so good that he came close to comfort her. Sometimes, when she told her story, people looked concerned, but would seldom grab her hand and give her the simple gesture of compassion. She knew Allen was special because he was showing her that his words were true. So, Nyssa pulled him close and gave him a big hug. She just clung to him and cried her eyes out. Allen could tell she needed it; he rubbed her back and encouraged her to let it out. Nyssa felt this was a breakthrough for her. She had some semblance of being normal in her life. She was no longer going to be a basket case, but a fighter instead. Starting tonight, she was going to begin the process of living her life to the fullest. Why not, here she was with the person she cared for the most, and he was willing to walk this walk with her. That brought a comfort that she couldn't even explain.

Quietly, Nyssa thanked God for the ability to know that he was working in her life. It was so hard to have HIV and to feel like God was working things out for her good. No longer having it would be the ultimate proof of God working things out, but He was in charge no matter how she felt about it. She knew she trusted Him when things were going great and questioned Him when it wasn't going the way she wanted it to. But, now that God was giving her a peek into his plan, by having Allen stand by her side as she took on this enemy with all her might, she felt fully ready to take it on with all her heart.

"Nyssa, I am so sorry to hear that. What a powerful story and tragic in the sense that you were a victim in this situation. To receive HIV in the manner you did is hard to fathom. To basically not play a part in the conception of it, but still have to deal with it nonetheless is disheartening. I want you to know that I am so proud of you. Knowing what I know now and seeing you carry yourself with grace and dignity every day shows strength and courage. I think back to our first couple of months talking, I would have never guessed you were facing anything other than day to day things. I am truly impressed, and I want you to know that I couldn't be happier to be with you."

"It has been an everyday struggle, but thank you God, for giving me everything I need."

"I do have a serious question to ask you."

"I feel like I can handle any question you have at this point," Nyssa said, feeling relieved after finally getting all that off her chest.

"Why did you take off running like you stole my wallet or something? I didn't know you had all that speed and grace in you, but when I saw you stumble I realized it might not be in you after all." Allen tried to get her to laugh to break up the seriousness of their conversation.

"Oh wow, you saw that? I ran like someone being chased in a b-rated scary movie. I tried to be sexy, but I guess my attempt to make you want me more didn't work."

"Oh, it worked. I thought of you the whole night as I kept laughing at the sight of you running in place like a cartoon. Thanks for that, because I will never let you forget it," Allen said as he kissed the back of Nyssa's hand.

"I didn't know what else to do. It was almost 'fight or flight' for me. I didn't know what to expect from you. I was scared that you might lash out at me or try to hurt me. I have had some terrible experiences when people found out I had HIV, and I couldn't handle heartbreak from you, so I ran off and disconnected my phone number."

"That was nice touch. You are so smart, so sexy," Allen said as they burst out laughing. "How was I supposed to call you since you disconnected your cell phone?"

"I don't know, smoke screen or by pigeon maybe. You are so good at the internet; you could have just sent me an email, genius."

"Touché." Allen chuckled and nodded in agreement. "I was so hurt when you ran off and left. I had it all planned out for the day you finally told me your secret. I was going to sit you down and look you in the eye and say, 'I am here for you'. I was going to let you know that you had a friend, a confidant, and someone who would support you. I wasn't going to let you feel alone and helpless like my friend Nathan did. He was torn up on the inside that all of our closest friends pretended like he didn't exist. Some blocked his number, some told him it was best that he not call them anymore, and some of them talked to him on the phone only, but made up every excuse about why they wouldn't come and visit him. I could never picture myself treating you that way. It would hurt me more than it would hurt you, probably, and I know how rewarding it is to be the kind of person that is there until the end. As sad as it was to see my boy go, it was great to have been there for him through thick and thin. The look on his face every time I showed up to visit kept me coming back, and I would do the same for you."

"I appreciate that so much, Allen. I have never asked much of the people I told about my situation. I just wanted them to continue to care for me regardless of what they'd just found out. Fear caused them to run because they probably felt, if I breathed on them they would get HIV. All I wanted was for them to accept me as a person. But, all I ever got was a shot of them running out the door."

"Don't worry, you will not experience that from me. You will be bombarded with support, prayers, and love."

"If you do that, then I will owe you more than life itself. I feel much better now that I've opened up to you. I tell you what, now that I've gotten all that out in the open, I really want to eat. I wasn't able to eat much all day long, and I am hungry. Please tell me you have more than coffee cake in this bootleg coffee shop you have. You have two flavors of coffee and no real food. Who does that? Even those major chains have sandwiches," Nyssa joked.

"Bootlegged? I will take that from you because you are fine. If you would stop in and look at the menu, then you will see we have over thirty domestic and fifteen international flavors. Not only that, but we have more than coffee cake—over twenty flavors of cake, actually. We do have sandwiches, but we also have soups, wraps, and other sweets like cookies, pastries, and crepes. But of course, you only come to the door to receive your free cup of coffee instead of sitting down and seeing how complex my shop's menu is. Just like our people always wanting a hook up."

"Believe me, your nasty coffee is not a hook up. I hate that you and your coffee are a package deal," Nyssa said as Allen burst into laughter.

"You are too much. So where do you want to go?"

"Hey, I know this spot on the beach that plays jazz music," Nyssa said, barely able to get it out without laughing.

"No way, never. That place was supposed to be our special place, but now it will be known as the place where you ran like a wounded gazelle. Let's just eat here."

"Okay, I like when you take charge, Allen. Not like that wimpy stalker that called me on Friday and asked me to go out."

"How is this for taking charge?" Allen said, standing and pulling Nyssa up as well. He pulled her close and kissed her passionately. Nyssa couldn't believe the kiss was happening, but she wasn't going to fight it. This was a real kiss, and Allen wasn't holding back. There was no hesitation with him. So, she let their kiss heal her heart of so much pain. To have him freely kiss her was beyond comforting.

Nyssa tried her best not to get emotional, but she couldn't help it. No one could have told her this would ever happen again and make her believe it.

Over the past three years, this scenario played out in her dreams, but not in reality. She couldn't imagine anyone treating her this way. To purposely kiss her and overlook the obvious, but to do it with such care was pure joy. She felt like a leper; she felt like everyone was afraid of her. She felt like no one would love her, but she was wrong. Allen loved her because only love would make someone overlook something as serious as HIV. She loved him because it was impossible to not love someone whose heart was this big. This was like an out of body experience; the kiss was putting her in a place that only love could reside in. The thought of that made her heart leap with joy.

5

Nyssa didn't understand why she couldn't sit up or move her arms and legs. She tried, but didn't have the ability. No command from her brain to her body was followed. Her breathing quickened, and for a second, she felt like she couldn't breathe. This made her heart start beating faster. She felt paralyzed and that scared her beyond measure.

Nyssa could tell she was asleep, but she felt a strange urge to wake up. She could hear three different beeps and muffled conversations. She tried to focus her attention on trying to open her eyes, but they felt like they were glued shut. The darkness was scaring her, and she felt afraid of it for the first time since she was a child.

It was that fateful night when her mom left her alone as she packed her things and left before Nyssa's father made it home from work. That was the night her mom left and never came back. Nyssa tried to scream out, but she couldn't open her mouth. What is going on? Her mind gave the command, but her jaw wouldn't listen. So, instead she began to focus on opening her eyes so the darkness would go away. She was determined to get them open. She could feel her eyelids start to flutter ever so slowly. The glare from the overhead light was blinding. Once her eyes adjusted to the light, she could see five people in green scrubs with surgical masks on standing over her. They weren't doing anything, but staring as if they were waiting on her next move. They reminded her of one of those creepy 80's science fiction movies. It was something so familiar about their eyes, but Nyssa didn't care about that. The fear in her heart was making it too hard for her to focus on any one thing.

This fear she felt was very familiar, and there was a tinge of déjà vu. Nyssa tried her hardest to get up or move, but she realized she was tied down by three large leather straps across her body, holding her in place. Her heart raced and sweat was trickling like water down her face. The harder she struggled the more the people standing over her began to smile. It sent a creepy shiver down her body as she wondered why they were grinning at her struggle.

All of a sudden, the people stopped laughing and walked about ten feet away from her. They huddled together and were whispering amongst themselves. Nyssa began to look around for any sharp objects or to see if anyone else was in the room that she could get help from. She immediately regretted looking around because the walls were covered with spiders of all shapes and sizes. They were crawling all over each other. Her number one phobia was spiders. The last thing she wanted was for them to get on her, because if they did, she wouldn't be able to do anything to get them off.

Nyssa found it hard to catch her breath. She wanted to focus on her breathing, to control it, but the thought of the spiders kept her from truly being able to concentrate. All she could think of was one of the spiders getting on her and biting her. The five-people stopped huddling and walked back towards her. They stood over her again, and one-by-one, began to remove their surgical masks. The first person was Mr. Manzini, her mentor at the Swaziland HIV Foundation. Nyssa couldn't understand why he would feel the need to operate on her. She loved Mr. Manzini like a father and trusted him, but she hadn't seen him in three years—since the accident. Besides, he wasn't a surgical doctor.

The next one was Rachel, her best friend. Nyssa felt let down that she would be here, letting this happen to her. After all, Rachel knew her fear of spiders and would never let Nyssa be in a room surrounded by them. And she was nowhere near, qualified to do surgery; yet, she stood here as if she was about to assist in one. The third person was her father. She felt that hurt to her heart. All her life, he had been there protecting and nurturing her, and now he was going to be a part of something so evil. Nyssa just couldn't understand why. She wanted to cry out 'Daddy!', but she couldn't open her mouth. Nyssa started to cry at the disappointment she felt toward father's participation in this.

The fourth person was Allen, and Nyssa was shocked beyond belief. After finally trusting him, and letting him in her life, how could he betray her? Was he getting her back for not telling him the truth? Did he want her to think that everything was okay so he could trick her into letting her guard down? The fifth person walked away before they removed their mask. Nyssa let her eyes follow the fifth person. There wasn't anyone close enough in her life to be a part of the four that had already made themselves known. The fifth person walked over to the nearest wall and reached into a mass of spiders.

Spiders fell all over the floor, and Nyssa watched in horror to make sure none ran towards her. Spiders crawled all over the equipment in the room. They started to cover every piece of equipment like they had covered the walls. The fifth person pulled out a jar that contained a dark red liquid from the wall of spiders. As the person walked back towards Nyssa, she noticed a large label on the jar that read 'HIV'. Nyssa began to thrash violently against her restraints. Mr. Manzini, Rachel, Nyssa's father, and Allen began to laugh uncontrollably as Nyssa fought to break free. These were the people she loved the most in life, and they were not willing to help her at all. Instead, they are laughing at her suffering.

The last person walked up and removed her mask. It was Nyssa's mother. At the sight of her mom, Nyssa immediately stopped crying and became very angry—an anger she couldn't control. Nyssa's mom got closer with the jar of blood, smiling a sinister smile. Nyssa wanted to give her mom a sharp piece of her mind, but she still wasn't able to speak. Her mom unscrewed the lid on the jar. Everyone else began to clap with great excitement. Nyssa's mom stood over her, near her head, and leaned it over so the blood poured out onto Nyssa's face. Nyssa watched helplessly as the blood began to pour over the lip of the jar. She closed her eyes tightly before the blood landed on her face. Nyssa tried to hold her breath so none of the blood got in her mouth. She held her breath for as long as she could, but

Enemy Inside of Me

Nyssa needed to catch a quick breath through her nose. She tried, but immediately began to choke on blood as it went in her nose. She was left with no choice but to breathe through her mouth. She gasped and coughed as blood went down her throat. She swallowed some, which only sent her into a fit of more coughing. All of a sudden, Nyssa could feel the straps loosening around her arms.

Since her arms were free, she frantically tried to wipe the blood off her face. As soon as the blood was out of her eyes, Nyssa could see that she was still on the operating table, but she was no longer in that scary, spider-covered room. She was now on a Swaziland road surrounded by taxis moving at a high rate of speed. Nyssa looked down; she was still strapped to the table by her waist and her legs. Nyssa could feel the African heat and smell the familiar smells of the area. Nyssa finally realized that, not only were the taxis moving fast, but so was she. She was moving, but she didn't know how.

She looked over her head and saw Ben, her taxi driver from the wreck, pushing her on the operating table down the street. He was smiling at her. Nyssa's anger rose again at the sight of him. She'd held onto so much unrepentant anger toward Ben because she felt that all of this could have been avoided if he had just driven a little more carefully instead of asking her all those distracting questions. Nyssa felt he should have spent more time focusing on the road than putting her through an interrogation. Now, here he was pushing her down the same street, once again, with no apparent regard for her safety. Nyssa wanted to scream at him to stop, but once again, she couldn't talk—which only fueled her anger. She was able to swallow HIV tainted blood, but she couldn't muster one word. Nyssa looked forward again because she was sick of seeing Ben's smile. She watched taxis pass them by, and every driver of every taxi was Ben. Once they passed the Swaziland HIV Foundation, a feeling of déjà vu came over her again.

It was only about a mile before they reached the scene of her accident. As the spot got closer and closer, Nyssa could hear Ben laughing. She quickly looked overhead to see why he was laughing. There was a taxi coming towards them, in their lane, and it was coming fast. Nyssa wanted to scream, but she couldn't. As the taxi came closer, Nyssa's heart was beating out of her chest. She knew there was no way they were going to avoid this collision. So, the taxi barreled closer, and Nyssa could see the driver's face clearly—Ben. He wore an evil grin. Right before they made contact, she tried to close her eyes, but her body adamantly rejected the command of her mind. Something wanted her to see this accident.

The taxi was only mere feet from her before she was able to let out a scream. The sound of her own voice woke her from the nightmare right before impact with the taxi. She immediately looked around to make sure she wasn't back in that spider covered room. She felt instant relief when she realized she was back in her bedroom. Her shirt was soaked with sweat, and her breathing was still quick. Nyssa was so relieved it was all a dream. She thought back over what took place in the dream and found herself momentarily mad at Mr. Manzini, Rachel, her father, and Allen for the role they'd played. She had to shake her head because she knew it wasn't right to be mad at them for being in her nightmare. She still felt some kind of way towards her mom and Ben, though. Even though she wanted to give them the same benefit of the doubt she gave the others, she couldn't. She was truly mad at them and that anger put her in a place she didn't want to be. Nyssa looked over at her clock and it read: 3:36am.

"Really Nyssa?" She said, flipping her pillow over and laying back down. She didn't have to be up for a few more hours and wanted to get as much sleep as possible. She felt drained from that nightmare, so there was an extra incentive to go back to sleep. Nyssa tried to close her eyes and go back to sleep, but she felt like it would be useless to try. So, she got up and walked over to her desk, turning on her laptop. She chugged a bottle of water she had left on her desk as she realized how extremely thirsty she was. As she waited for her laptop to boot up, she couldn't help thinking about the weird nightmare. It was as if everyone she loved had betrayed her, but she knew that was so far from the truth. They had all been 100% supportive of Nyssa, actually doing more than what was expected of them. They all took time to ensure she knew they loved her and would always be there for her. Everyone had her back, and then some—everyone except her mom.

Now, Nyssa felt like her mom would definitely be evil and give her HIV, especially since she had never shown any love towards Nyssa at all. Her mom reacted just like she would have if that scenario was true. Nyssa didn't like the anger she harbored for her mom and the way it made her feel. She really didn't want to give her mom that much control over her. If there was a way for her to be erased from her memory, Nyssa would sign up to make that happen. Once her laptop was up and running, she opened up her email so she could send Allen a message as a surprise in the morning. After their talk over the past weekend, they had been closer than ever. They were now seeing each other twice a day—when Nyssa went to work and when she headed home. She had enjoyed the freedom of not hiding behind her disease, and because of that, she'd felt ten times happier than ever before. Her email opened, and she noticed a couple of new emails. One was from Mr. Manzini. Nyssa wanted to wait until after she sent Allen an email, but something was tugging at her to open this email first. It said:

> *Nyssa,*
> *I hope this email finds you in the grace of God as you live and breathe. I am sending this to inform you of our 30-year anniversary and the new program we are launching called "13 is only the beginning". This will take place in six months' time. I wanted to give you a heads up so you can make all the proper arrangements to attend if you are so inclined to do so. We have missed you these past three years and would love to show you our upgrades, and let you hear, firsthand, the testimonies of some of the children. Let me know if you plan on attending.*
> *Take care,*
> *Mr. Manzini*

Nyssa had a huge smile on her face while she read the email. A ton of memories came flooding back as she began to get emotional. She had let her diagnosis stop her from doing what was on her heart. She knew she shouldn't have let HIV stop her from living and doing what she loved. It had been three long years since the last time she stepped foot in Africa. She missed everyone and knew that she didn't want to miss the anniversary. Now that she had a new purpose and focus, Nyssa knew she was going to go, but felt like she would need some support. She forwarded the email to Rachel and asked if she would come as well. With Rachel by her side, Nyssa felt like she could handle the pressure of driving past the hospital where she was infected and the site of the crash. Rachel would know what to say and how to say it. Nyssa knew she would need that more than ever.

So, Nyssa put the date on her calendar and scheduled a reminder so she could look up flights later on. Now, she wanted to send Allen a little email to let him know she was thinking of him. She noticed there was another email she hadn't opened; it was from Allen. That made her heart leap with joy. She looked at the time, and it had come through right after they got off the phone last night. Talking to him the past couple of days had been less of a chore and more of a joy as she could freely talk about any and everything without worrying about what was asked or said. Now, she was excited to see what he sent her.

Miss Thorne,

I was wondering if you would like to join me on Friday, as a do-over for you totally ruining our date last Friday. In your haste to drink as much as you could and run away as fast as humanly possible, you took a night of promise and made it one of doubt. You no doubt owe me a do-over. So, accept this offer to be in my presence on Friday. I will arrange to have you picked up, so please make yourself available around 3pm. I do understand that is during your working hours, but be bold and do something bad for once in your boring life. Okay, I look forward to your response. Please send it as fast as you drank that white wine last week.

Allen

Nyssa couldn't help but burst out laughing. That was the sweetest email she had gotten in a long time. Allen really was a funny guy, and she knew she was blessed to have him. He was so much like her in many ways. She was more than happy to send him a reply.

To the owner of a crappy coffee shop,

I will accept your invitation to go out on Friday. It was funny how I was able to drink you under the table and still had the ability to out run you in sand. I will go out with you as you have no other options and out of the debt I owe society. I will take one for the team and be with you in public, even though you dress funny and have weak arms. Take this as a gift from me to you.

Sincerely,
The woman that is out of your league!

Nyssa had to laugh at her response. She loved the fact that she could just be herself without having to worry about holding back. Allen loved her sense of humor. She was free to be who she was and didn't have to worry about people expecting her to be serious all the time because she was a doctor. Nyssa was very different from the rest of the doctors at her office, and that was what her clients loved most about her. She was personable with each person. She made sure they could laugh and joke even though they were faced with serious illnesses. Nyssa shut down her email and walked back to her bed, plopping down onto the sheets. She grabbed her second pillow and hugged it tight. Nyssa let the thought of Allen, and how thankful she was for him, put her in a place of comfort and peace.

"How much farther?" Nyssa asked the Uber driver

as he sped down the road. Ever since they left her loft, he had been driving extremely fast. There were two reasons why she wanted to get out of the car. One, the Uber driver didn't believe that he should follow any road safety rules, such as a speed limit or yielding for others. It was as if his life was at stake if she didn't get to her destination as soon as possible. She thought maybe he had a great imagination and believed he was a secret agent who was being followed. Whatever the reason, she didn't feel safe, and she knew she would feel better when they safely arrived. Allen set up an Uber driver for her and asked her to just go along with his plan for the day.

The second reason she wanted to get out of the car was to see Allen. She knew that once she made it to her destination, hopefully in one piece, she would be face-to-face with the one person that had been able to get to Nyssa's heart. In only five months, he had brought on feelings of love that she thought were a figment of her imagination. She felt like the only romance that would come her way would be in the movies she watched. It was strange for her to feel this way. It was as if this was that old high school love where, the very first time you had strong feelings for someone, it made you think you were going to be with that person forever. She was enjoying the fact that she looked forward to seeing him and knowing he felt the same way made it that much more enjoyable.

The way they were approaching this delicate situation was by making it a more comfortable transition. They both knew that Nyssa had HIV, so there had to be a mode of caution with it, but it also gave them a chance to experience the purity of dating the old-fashioned way— getting to know someone fully before taking an intimate step. It was reassuring to know that they could completely focus on other aspects of their relationship besides intimacy. The mature approach they had towards dating each other was what brought life to each conversation. In this day and age, talks amongst people were about material things or complaints about life itself. But, they talked about life, politics, nature, and God. No need to constantly talk about what they wanted in a relationship, but they talked about the fullness of getting to know one another on a spiritual level—which is lacking in most relationships.

Nyssa had enjoyed sharing each other's experiences in life. They had shared childhood stories, mistakes, and accomplishments. Nyssa was opening up to Allen because she felt so comfortable with him. She felt that it was easy to share with him because of his replies. He was not judgmental or preachy when it came to questioning why she did this or that. He just listened to her, and that was something she enjoyed. He made her feel like everything she said was something he desperately wanted to hear. He was a great listener and that was a unique quality in a man.

"We are almost there, ma'am," the Uber driver said as he turned around to speak to Nyssa. She grew more nervous as she felt that he stayed turned around a few seconds to long; he could have easily gotten into an accident, and that immediately put a tinge of fear in her as she recalled Ben doing the same thing on that fateful day.

"Okay," Nyssa said as she double checked her seat belt for a little bit of reassurance. Nyssa wasn't too familiar with the area. She heard about how nice it was, but it was an expensive area of town. Not that price had ever been an issue, but she limited purchases to clothes mainly—as most women do.

"Okay, here we are," the Uber driver announced as he turned into a subdivision with a security guard on duty. The security guard motioned for them to drive forward.

"Hi, who are you here to see?" The security guard asked as the car came to a stop at the gate. The Uber driver looked back at Nyssa for an answer, but all he got was a 'deer in the headlights' look.

"Umm, how about Allen?"

"Oh, that annoying guy that keeps calling up here asking about a young lady that is supposed to be dropped off. You get out here Miss," The security said as he lifted the gate arm up. "Driver, just make a U-turn at that junction right there and go ahead on out."

"Thank you, sir," Nyssa said as she climbed out of the car. She was greeted by a warm 85-degree breeze. It felt good flowing through her hair, which she had down for this occasion. As the Uber driver made his U-turn, Allen came walking up right on time.

Allen was nervous as he walked back to the front gate to wait on Nyssa to arrive. He would have just brought her, but he wanted to look over the Airbnb himself. He wanted to make sure it was super clean, but also that it had everything the listing said it would have. After all, he took off on a Friday for the first time since he'd opened the coffee shop, so he wanted to make sure everything went off without a hitch. He wanted to impress Nyssa and make this special. Allen was so happy he didn't have to pretend about not knowing Nyssa's situation anymore. He didn't necessarily like deceiving her, but he didn't know what else to do. The whole time he kept the secret from her, he imagined how he would feel if he had HIV. Would he tell everyone he met? Would he wait like she did until she knew and trusted them?

He knew it must have been eating Nyssa up on the inside, to really care for someone and have to risk the chance of losing them by sharing a secret like that. Then to find out how she received HIV was even more heartbreaking. His heart went out to her. She had been saddled with a disease that was normally associated with bad behavior. Allen could almost understand her plight because his friend Nathan suffered the same pain, but worse because his HIV advanced to AIDS. The way people treated Nathan upset Allen so much. Nathan would have given the shirt off his back for any of the friends that abandoned him. Everyone acted as if he was too sick to visit or way too contagious to touch. Allen and Nathan's mom were the only people willing to be by his side. It was disheartening. Allen knew that he would never abandon Nathan, and he wasn't going to abandon Nyssa either.

He knew that, in order for their relationship to work, they must be careful with how they approached things. Two perfectly healthy adults could do just about anything they wanted with each other, but when one person was sick and one wasn't, it brought on a whole new dynamic. Allen knew he was willing to do all he could to ensure that their relationship wasn't hindered in anyway just because of what they faced. All he knew was that he truly cared for Nyssa and wanted to be as supportive as possible. Allen realized that, as their relationship became more public and people found out about her having HIV, they would ask him why he was willing to risk his life to be with her. He didn't care what they thought, because his level of care for Nyssa overrode their feelings. In Allen's mind, why wouldn't Nyssa deserve to be loved, regardless of her situation?

Do people truly believe in love or do they believe in love when it benefits them? How about loving someone to the point where they were the focus of your love, as a blessing to them? Allen felt like Nyssa deserved compassion, and above all, she deserved unconditional love. People don't truly display unconditional love anymore, because if they did, it would be seen on a daily basis. Nyssa didn't ask for HIV, nor did she deserve it; so, Allen wanted to bless her with a love that was from God. Jesus sacrificed his life so we could have eternal life, and that love he gave was so special. We didn't deserve it, but we needed it. Allen would love Nyssa because she needed to be loved after all she had been through. And no one was going to talk him out of it.

So, all things were in place, and now he needed to hurry to be at the gate when Nyssa arrived. Soon as he walked up, he noticed the guard talking to the Uber driver. His app showed the car had arrived. Allen had missed her this morning when she came to get her morning coffee. He waited until the Uber drive made his U-turn before walking towards Nyssa. He looked at her and couldn't understand why someone so fine wanted to be with him. Her looks were captivating. She was by far the prettiest woman around. There wasn't anyone as naturally pretty as Nyssa, in Allen's opinion. Nyssa looked up and saw Allen walking towards her. She couldn't wait to give him a big hug—because she was happy to have made it safely and because she'd missed him this morning. The thought of missing him just made seeing him that much more special.

"Hi Miss Thorne. Thank you for coming," Allen

said as he walked up and kissed Nyssa on the lips.

"Hey Allen." Nyssa gave him the hug she had been waiting to give him all day.

"I would have brought you here myself, but I needed to prepare everything we are going to do today. You won't need an Uber again. I am bringing you back."

"Well, I understand, but next time just bring me. You could have saved me from the heart attack I almost had with Speed Racer driving like there was no tomorrow."

"I didn't want to ruin the surprise. That is… if you like this kind of surprise." Allen said as he grabbed Nyssa's right hand.

"If I don't, you will know. I cleared my schedule for this so it better be magical, or I will put you on blast online for not meeting my high standards," Nyssa said as she squeezed Allen's hand and held on tight.

"You look so pretty today. Every time I see you, you remind me of how God makes such beautiful things. I really like the dress you have on today. It's nice and shape-hugging," Allen complimented, referring to the white summer dress she had on with large red roses on it. The cotton texture to was very soft and made it thick enough to hide the swimsuit she had on underneath.

"Thanks, I wore this beautiful dress for you, and I see you dressed like you were going to cut the grass in your yard. No, I am just playing. You look good," Nyssa said, winking at Allen. Allen had on some long gray swimming trunks that came down to his knees and a black t-shirt with a large white cross on the front.

"Wow, cutting grass? You are silly."

"You love me."

"More than you know, Nyssa. Come this way,

right through here," Allen said as he guided her down the sidewalk. There was a long sidewalk that leads to an open field, but it was through some thick trees that shielded the view of what was on the other side. The path started out shaded at the opening, but as she looked ahead, it was less so. The trees were not as dense as before, because Nyssa was able to see more sunlight coming through. She could faintly see something black moving up ahead between the leaves. They kept on walking, and when they reached the end of sidewalk, there was a large clearing. It dead-ended right to a wood fence. Tied to the fence was a beautiful black horse. Its black coat shone in the sunlight.

Beyond the horse was a large field that was nothing but open land. The field went a long way, at least a mile or so, and it looked like it was well kept. Nyssa could see the trees that surrounded the field on the right and left. She was a sucker for nature and animals too. While she was admiring the scene, Allen walked over to the horse, untied it, and began petting it. He then grabbed the reins and pulled the horse towards Nyssa. Allen had never looked more handsome than when he was walking up with the horse.

"What a beautiful horse! What's its name?"

"Midnight. How do you feel about horses?" Allen asked, giving the horse a firm pat on the neck

"I have never ridden a horse before."

"What? You have been living in Texas all these years, and you've never ridden a horse. How could you? Well, I guess today will be a day of firsts," Allen said as a look of excitement flashed across his face.

"Whatever, ole country bumpkin. Don't get all wild, wild west on me, because you are more city-like than me,"

Nyssa said, shaking her head at Allen. She'd never even thought about riding a horse before, but she figured it would be romantic to ride with Allen.

"Okay, I am going to get on the horse, then help you get on."

"Not with those puny arms. My bad, I shouldn't talk about your weak arms. I know something is missing, though. Um... where is the saddle?"

"No saddle. We are going to go bareback. This will give you the full experience of riding a horse. It might hurt a little, but don't focus on it. I am used to it, so it doesn't bother me. I think you'll be fine," Allen said as he jumped on the horse and burst out laughing. Nyssa gave him a look like she didn't believe him.

"Okay, okay. I forgot to get a saddle, you happy? It might hurt a little, but as you tell me, 'don't be a wimp'. So, you don't get to be one either," Allen said as he stretched both of his hands out to the left, towards Nyssa. Nyssa put the bag she was carrying on her back and grabbed his hands.

"Okay, I am going to pull you up, and as I do that, give yourself a nice jump to help. If you give me one big leap, you should be safely on. On the count of three... one, two, three!" Allen pulled real hard as Nyssa jumped and landed on the horse behind him. She took a moment to balance herself.

"You can hold onto my waist," Allen suggested. Nyssa wrapped her arms around him and could feel how hard his ab muscles were.

"Okay Mr. Five-Minute Abs. You might be working with something."

"I am going to ignore you. Are you ready?"

"I think so. I hope you can control this beast."

"Don't be scared. You will be fine, I promise," Allen said as he put a hand on top of her right hand. Nyssa knew she would be fine, but it was always the unknown that was hardest to be comfortable with. Allen looked back at her and smiled. He then removed his hand from hers and grabbed the reins. Giving them a jerk motion up and down, the horse began to walk. Nyssa held on a little tighter. Allen just laughed as the horse started walking a little faster. Then all of a sudden, Allen jerked the reins again up and down, and the horse began to run. Nyssa squeezed her arms even tighter around Allen's middle because she was bouncing all over the place. It took her a few yards before she was able to fully gain balance. Allen slowed the horse down a few strides later.

"If you just sit up straight and hang on real tight, you will be able to enjoy the ride. To keep from bouncing up and down excessively, hug the horse with your legs. Keep your posture and you will be able to keep your balance," Allen instructed. She nodded in response, and he jerked the reins up and down causing them to take off again. True to his word, after a minute of riding, she was able to follow his instructions enough to keep her balance. She was starting to enjoy the ride a little more. She never thought she would like riding horses, but she was enjoying herself so far.

It was something about riding the horse that made her appreciate God. She was able to look around and check out the scenery. This was one of God's creations that she never had the chance to really get to know and enjoy. She could feel the thump of the horse's hooves when they touched the ground. Riding the horse with Allen made the experience that much greater. There was something special about riding a horse and enjoying a great view that put things into perspective. Riding the horse with Allen had a romantic feel to it, just like in those romance novels where the handsome prince comes and sweeps the princess off her feet. They would ride off into the sunset together and all the people in the land would cheer them on.

Her heart was definitely the one cheering this scenario. It was definitely a surprise and she relished it. Allen had total control of the horse as they soared through the field. Nyssa smiled because she didn't think Allen had it in him to plan this, or even know how to ride a horse. The beauty about getting to know someone was the fact that you find out interesting skills that often aren't seen on the surface. They slowed down and Nyssa realized she was a little disappointed that it was over already. Once the horse came to a stop, Allen turned around to face her.

"Hey, let me teach you how to ride. Is that cool with you?" Allen asked.

"I would love to learn," Nyssa said, feeling nervous and excited at the same time. Allen jumped off and motioned for Nyssa to slide forward. Once she had, Allen jumped back on the horse behind Nyssa.

"Okay, all you have to do is make sure you are in control. A horse can feel when you are nervous, and sometimes they don't respond well to that. Don't you worry, because I am going to teach you the basics and you will be totally fine," Allen said as he instructed Nyssa on the basic commands. Nyssa made sure she listened closely because she was afraid of being thrown off.

"Okay, whenever you're ready. I am going to hold you tight just in case."

"That's what I am talking about, but it will cost you.

No one hugs me like that for free," Nyssa said welcoming his hands around her. Once Allen grabbed her waist, she did as she was instructed. She loved the way the horse responded to her; it was exhilarating. She was shocked at the control she had, and the courage she was showing, because she had no problem making the horse run faster. The thrill of riding was something she was never going to forget. They rode around the field about five times as Nyssa realized she just couldn't get enough of this moment. She began to slow the horse down.

"What's up? I thought you were having fun?"

"Oh I am, but I was just going to ask you about us swimming." She hadn't seen a swimming pool or even a body of water the whole time they were riding around the field.

"Are you ready to go swimming?"

"I am."

"Okay, take us that way until you come to the end of the field."

"Okay." Nyssa commanded the horse to move again until he was running. As they were racing through the field, Nyssa took a glance up ahead. She thought she could see more trees, as if they were getting to the end of the field. Nyssa slowed the horse to a nice trot. She intently watched, waiting to see what was ahead. They were getting closer to the end of the field, but not necessarily getting closer to the trees. Nyssa thought that was odd. The distance between the trees was not getting shorter. So, when they got close enough, she realized that the field dead-ended to what looked like a cliff. The trees were on the other side, on another cliff. She slowed the horse down until he was at an easy walk.

"Okay, we can get off here. Just pick which side of the horse you want to get off on, swing the opposite leg over to that side, and slide off. Here hold on to me," Allen said as he reached his arm out for her to hang on to. Nyssa got off the horse as gracefully as possible. Allen jumped off like a professional. "Give me a second to put up Midnight in the stable right over there, and I will be right back." Allen pointed to a clearing on the left side of the field. Not too far off was a brown stable that looked very well kept.

"Okay, where are we?"

"We are at a popular and expensive Airbnb community. It is similar to a time share, but way better. You not only get access to a house, but you also get access to all the land and things on it. A group of owners that have establishments around the museum, partnered up to buy properties here. Another owner and I went in half on a house. So, we share, but he comes out here way more than I do because he can golf. I don't come that often. Anyway, let me put Midnight up." Nyssa took out her cell phone and took some pictures. She watched Allen walk off to the stable.

Allen closed the stable door and walked back towards Nyssa.

"Okay. So, what now?" Nyssa asked.

"Come with me." Allen grabbed Nyssa's hand and walked towards the end of the field. She was able to see a large body of water that separated them from the other side of the cliff. The water was so blue and clear, it looked very inviting on this warm spring day. Nyssa was scared to walk all the way to the edge because there was a steep drop of about fifteen feet to the water. On the right and left side of the body of water was white sand. The distance between the two sides was about two hundred feet. There were five bamboo beach chairs with large umbrellas on both sides of the water, as well as three eight-foot tall huts. There was a six-foot-long, and six-foot-wide section of boards that looked like some sort of raft with a palm tree in the middle. It looked like something you could put in the water and float on. Nyssa knew this was a manmade beach, and from the looks of it, very exclusive.

So, they got to the very edge of the field, and Nyssa looked over the side wondering how they were going to get down. She looked over at the other cliff and could see that there were stairs leading down to the beach, but on their side, there was nothing.

"Great view huh? That is where we're going. Did you bring your swimsuit?"

"I have my swimsuit on under my dress. The view is very nice, but how are we going to get down?"

"I thought that was obvious. We're going to jump," Allen said smiling.

"What? I am not going to jump down there. How do you know I can swim?" Nyssa asked. She was afraid of the prospect of jumping down to the water.

"You mentioned swimming as a little girl. I can recall you talking about how that swimming pool water was murder on your hair, and you were embarrassed seeing pictures of yourself."

"That still doesn't mean I am going to jump."

"Nyssa, we came all this way, and you are going to back out now?"

"Why didn't we just come here from that side? That side has stairs…" Nyssa asked, pointing to the other cliff.

"For one, we would not have been able to ride Midnight, and two, I want to see what you're made of."

Nyssa took another glance over the side, then backed up from the edge.

"What about my bag? My cellphone, keys, and my gun are in there. I can't get them wet." Nyssa was searching for any reason not to jump down into the water.

"You don't have a gun. Wait… knowing you, you might."

"I need one since you turned this day into a western with us riding horses and jumping off cliffs and such."

Allen laughed as he walked towards the edge and stopped a few feet from it. At his feet was a rope that came out of the ground and hung over the side of the cliff. Allen pulled the rope up until he got to the end. On the end of the rope was a small square object that looked like some sort of float.

"We are going to put your bag on here, along with our clothes and shoes. I am then going to lower this down to the water, and it will be waiting on us when we get down."

Nyssa knew she was running out of excuses, and it looked like Allen was not going to back down.

"What if I don't jump?" Nyssa asked as her mind raced for another excuse not to jump.

"Nyssa, come on. Look fear in the face and remember that this is a moment you cannot get back. If you chicken out now, you will have missed out on the opportunity of a lifetime. So far, you have been real good with trusting me, and all I ask is that you trust me again." Nyssa didn't want to disappoint him.

"Okay," Nyssa agreed hesitantly.

"Great!" Allen put the float down and took off his black Nike cross trainers. Then, with no hesitation, took off his shirt. Nyssa wanted to look away, but she couldn't. She took a peek at his chest and definitely liked what she saw. He was athletically built, like a track star, and she was quite surprised that he was as muscular as he was—seeing that he said he rarely worked out. She watched him put his shirt and shoes on the float. He then stood up and looked at her.

"Sometime today, while we're still young," Allen said, waiting on her to take off her dress. Nyssa quickly slipped out of the sundress she was wearing. The warm sun was soothing to her skin. She wasn't worried about how she looked in the two-piece because she knew she killed it with the shape she was in. She folded up the dress and handed it to him.

"Wow. Nyssa, you look good. Nice abs."

"Pilates."

"Nice. Real nice," Allen said as he grabbed the sundress from her and placed it on the float. There were two straps hanging off that he used to secure their things. He made a real nice bow on top. He then picked up the float and walked towards the edge. He grabbed the rope and lowered the float until it landed safely on top of the water. Nyssa just stood there scared, because she realized that in a few seconds, she was going to have to jump. Once the float was on the water, Allen immediately looked back at Nyssa.

"There are two ways we can do this. I can jump in first and show you that everything is okay, but then you are going to have to talk yourself off the ledge…literally. Your second option is that we hold hands and jump in at the same time. Which one sounds best to you?"

"The stairs sound best to me, but that wasn't an option. Let's hold hands and jump together," Nyssa said, feeling that was the wiser choice. She knew there was no way she could talk herself into jumping on her own.

"Okay then, let's do it. We are going to do it with no hesitation. If I let you decide, we will probably waste this whole day. On the count of three, we are going to just take off running and jump. Okay?" Allen grabbed Nyssa's left hand and walked them from the cliff about five feet. Nyssa could feel her heart pounding. The moment was coming, and there was nothing she could do about it.

"One..."

Nyssa felt like throwing up. She started laughing nervously as she pictured herself throwing up her pancakes as they jumped over the cliff.

"Two..."

Now her knees felt like giving way, and she had a good mind to just let Allen drag her over the edge.

"Three!" Allen took off running and had to literally pull Nyssa towards the edge of the cliff. Nyssa took a couple of steps, and before she knew it, she was looking down. Allen pulled her the last foot over the side, and Nyssa had well enough sense to plant her last step and jump, because she didn't want to do a belly flop from fifteen feet up. She immediately closed her eyes and screamed at the top of her lungs. She felt gravity pulling them down, and it felt like an eternity before they finally hit the water. The coolness of it covered her body as she went below the surface. She welcomed the touch of the water and was happy that her mini flight was over. She opened her eyes and could see the bottom of the lake about five feet from them. Allen let go of her hand, and they swam to the top. She was excited that she had in fact jumped into the water. She looked up at the cliff. From the water, it didn't look as scary as it did from cliff level.

"Yes, I did it!" Nyssa screamed like an excited little kid. She looked over at Allen who was just smiling at her.

"I knew you could do it, and don't you feel better

now that you've jumped in?"

"I do! I don't think I want to do it again, but I'm glad I did it once," Nyssa said swimming up to Allen.

"Okay. I will go get the float and will meet you in the shallow part." Nyssa began swimming towards the beach, and she could still feel her heart beating fast. She was extremely proud of herself for jumping even if she had to be coaxed into doing it. She swam underwater and was so impressed with how clear it was. She could see the bottom and the slope it took leading up to the beach. She looked behind her and could see Allen swimming on top of the water, with the float, not too far behind. So, she surfaced and looked at the beach. Once she made it to the shallow part, she touched the ground with her feet, and stood up.

She walked the rest of the way until she was out of the water. She saw the five bamboo beach chairs with large umbrellas, and three bamboo huts—one was a men's restroom and one was for women. The third hut had two white refrigerators in it. Nyssa walked to the dry sand and turned around to see Allen carrying the float out of the water. She tried not to look at his body as he passed by, but she couldn't help herself. She watched him set the float on the sand near one of the bamboo beach chairs.

"What other deadly challenges do you have for us now? Are you going to release a gang of sharks?" Nyssa asked playfully.

"I am glad you asked. We are going to see who can collect the most gold coins. I am going to throw them in the water, and we have to get as many as we can. We'll add them up and whoever wins gets to decide what we do on our next outing."

"Who said I am going out with you again? You are crazy. I definitely can't let you win. You might have us fighting tigers or walking on hot coals." Nyssa knew she was very competitive and hated to lose. Losing to Allen would be something she would have to hear about for the rest of her life.

"Okay, so it's a deal then," Allen said, walking over to the hut with the refrigerators. He ducked behind the counter and pulled up a bowl of baseball size coins. Approaching the water, he just threw them all in. He walked back to the hut and dropped the bowl down on the ground, then ran passed Nyssa before diving into the water. Nyssa knew exactly what he was trying to pull.

"That is cheating!" Nyssa shouted as she laughed out loud.

Nyssa dove in the water after him and could immediately see the coins shining on the bottom of the lake. The water was so clear, that the sun sparkled on every piece. It was a beautiful sight to behold. There were at least twenty gold pieces glistening below. It looked like each coin had its own spotlight as the sun reflected off them. Nyssa quickly swan towards a group of coins away from Allen. She noticed that he was pretty quick at swimming, and so she knew he probably had way more than her already. But she loved the game, so she just played along. After a few minutes of gathering all the coins she could, she swam over to where Allen was standing. She could see that the pile of coins in his hands were twice as big as the few she could find.

"I know you won. For one, you cheated." They were now in about a foot of water.

"How did I cheat? I never told you any rules. I only said that I was going to throw them in the water, and we were going to have to go in and get them. I didn't say anything about starting at the same time." Allen winked at her.

"Oh okay. I stand corrected. You won fair and square so you get to choose what we do the next time we get together."

Nyssa wanted to win badly, but she knew she would enjoy whatever he decided.

"Since you are picking next time, let me choose something for us to do now. Let's play tag, and you are it, but I get a ten second head start." Without waiting for a response, Nyssa ran and dove into the water. She began to swim as fast as she could. She knew that there was no place for her to go but to the other side of the water, to the other beach. What was she going to do then, besides run around chairs or lock herself in the restroom? The beach was about two hundred feet from where she was, and she knew she wouldn't make it before being tagged. So, she began to slow down.

All of a sudden, she stopped swimming because she heard Allen dive in. He was swimming very fast behind her. She went deep underwater trying to think of what moves she could do to possibly get away from him. She watched Allen swim towards her and couldn't help but laugh—thus, releasing all of her breath. She immediately went to the surface, and Allen followed behind her. He touched her back on the way up.

"I am sorry. I couldn't help but laugh. I knew I had nowhere to go. I didn't think the game all the way through," Nyssa said between laughs. Allen just shook his head.

"It's okay. I must say that was the quickest game I have ever played."

Nyssa really started to laugh then, as she reached out and grabbed Allen. He pulled her close to him, and they swam back towards more shallow water. Once they got there, he stood up—the water coming up below his waist. Nyssa took a quick dip underwater because she wanted her hair to be slicked back and not on her face. When she came out of the water, it was like those commercials when the pretty woman steps out of the pool—water dripping off her body. Nyssa was glad for the numerous hours she'd spent working out. She knew that before this moment, she never really cared what someone thought about her. She truly cared what Allen thought, and for this moment's sake, she hoped he admired her.

He didn't say anything; he just stared at her. Nyssa watched his eyes move from her face, down to her stomach, and back up to her face. She didn't mind; his eyes told her all she needed to know, and she felt like he was pleased with what he could see. They just stood there for a few seconds more. Then, as if on cue, they moved towards each other, kissing passionately. It was as if the world was spinning around them. Nyssa wanted to give the thumbs up behind his back as she hugged him close to her, but she didn't. She silently did it in her mind as she was enjoying the kiss she had been waiting on since the peck he gave her when she arrived at the gate. She didn't consider that a kiss because it was nothing like this one. The kiss from earlier was quick, and it was over before it really began. This kiss here had feelings, and it was exactly what Nyssa thought it would be. She didn't know how long they were going to go with the kiss, but she made sure she did all she could to savor every second being in his arms. It felt like the Fourth of July, with explosions going off like magic in the background. For now,

Nyssa would settle for the explosion going off in her heart. A year ago, this day would have only been a dream, but now, because of the grace of God, it was a reality. Allen slowly pulled away first, grabbing her hand as they walked towards the beach area. He walked her to one of the bamboo beach chairs, offering her a seat. He then returned to the hut with the refrigerators in it.

"Would you like something to drink? They have tea and sodas."

"Any kind of fruit tea is fine with me," Nyssa replied as she sat back, replaying the kiss they just shared in her mind. She wanted to enjoy every moment from this point on as she relished living—not being so caught up in worrying about having HIV.

Allen grabbed a bottle of strawberry tea and a bottle of sweetened tea, then closed the refrigerator. He walked back to where Nyssa was sitting, opened her bottle of tea, and handed it to her.

"Thanks sweetheart."

"No problem," Allen said as he opened his bottle and sat down next to her.

This was the first time Nyssa really got a chance to look the area over, and she loved it. To have this small beach at their disposal was nice.

"This place is great. Thanks for bringing me here." As Nyssa looked over at Allen, she felt like their relationship was changing. In a way, it had. They went from being friends with secrets, to a slow developing relationship. Nyssa knew for a fact that she would never kiss a friend the way she just kissed him. That kiss put a stamp on how she felt about him, and she hoped he felt that.

"I love this place too. It is beautiful, quiet, and at the

moment, cozy," Allen said, chuckling.

"Why are you laughing?" Nyssa asked curiously.

"To make sure that you and I would be here alone, I sent an email from the Airbnb page to all other owners saying the beach was closed for repairs. I was being sneaky," Allen confessed as he really started to laugh at himself. Nyssa took it as a show of how he felt about her.

"I am glad you did that. I really am enjoying being with you, you big lying, cliff jumping, horse riding fool."

"I have wanted to spend time with you here since I first met you. After our talk, I feel like we need to do all we can to enjoy every moment together."

The sound of that gave Nyssa a rush of excitement. She was so happy that Allen felt that way because it was so similar to how she felt. He didn't know, but she could hardly sleep last night because she was so excited for what he had planned for today. He didn't disappoint her. As a matter of fact, Allen hadn't disappointed her at all in any form or fashion. He had been consistent, if nothing else, and she loved that about him.

"I wanted to see you when I picked up my coffee this morning, but I knew you were planning this, 'western staycation', so I figured I could wait. Who would have known that you would make this city girl happy by making my being-a-cowgirl dreams come true?"

"I bet you wanted to see me alright. You would have wanted to see me just long enough to get your coffee, and then you would have left faster than you came. You definitely have great taste in coffee, though. I like that about you."

"You didn't actually think I drink the coffee you give me every morning, did you? Man, I pour that out once I hit the parking lot. Haven't you noticed that huge brown spot out there? That's why I leave so fast. It's like a gag reflex my hand has. As soon as that coffee cup touches my hand, it quickly tries to throw it away. It's so weird how that happens," Nyssa said as she tried not to laugh.

"Ha-ha, you are so wrong, but at least I get to see you," Allen said shaking his head at Nyssa. He loved her sense of humor so much. He was really beginning to fall for her even more. Nyssa definitely felt the same way. Nothing else mattered to her. She had fully submerged herself in this moment and couldn't think of anything else. All she could think about was this wonderful Texas weather, beautiful private beach, and Allen.

"Allen, I want you to know that I have these feelings that I hid from you because of my sickness. They are strong, and I feel like they are growing stronger every day. I didn't think I would let myself feel this way for anyone again, but I do. It feels as if I don't have HIV the way you treat me, and that means so much to me. I say this because I don't want this to end when the newness of us starting this relationship wears off. I don't want to hold back my feelings for you, and I don't want to face the rest of my life without you."

"Me either. I have enjoyed our time together. The feelings I have for you are real and very deep. I know that you are dealing with a lot when it comes to this disease, but I want us to find a way to make it work. I want us to work on staying together. I know one major thing was that you didn't want to be hurt, and I can understand that. At the same time, we are mature enough to be able to handle this. We know how we feel towards each other. I know that I am not afraid of being with you because I care for you that much. I am willing to do whatever it takes for this relationship to work," Allen said as he smiled at Nyssa sincerely.

"It is so easy for me to be willing to give it a try, but the thing that scares me the most is that you are going to be dealing with family and friends that will not understand why you are with me. What happens if they turn their backs on you?" Nyssa asked. She was concerned about overbearing relatives that could make it hard for Allen to be with her.

"I understand that, but I am willing to take on any problem as long as I am with you, Nyssa. My heart is for you. When I found out you had HIV, I didn't blink or think twice. I knew I still wanted you, and I don't care what anyone says. I would still love them if they had HIV, so why wouldn't they want me to love you since you have it? I just know that I am so blessed to be able to share this life with you, disease and all. I am not leaving you, and that is that."

Nyssa would have given a kidney to hear anyone say that to her. The sorrow and pain of the last three years had taken a toll on her—to where she couldn't even hear from God. She had downgraded any blessing she was given because none of them compared to being totally healed from HIV. She could be honest with her feelings. She was so mad at God that she was no longer any good for the kingdom. She stopped going to church and stopped her outreach to Africa because she felt like God had failed her. All the while, God had already groomed Allen to be the one who would be there for her no matter what. God had already ordained her blessing, but she couldn't see it, and that was the beauty about God. Just because we don't know what He is doing, doesn't mean He isn't doing anything. He hadn't forsaken her, and He was working her situation out for her good even if she didn't believe so.

Seeing Allen now, reminded her of all the things she asked God to bring to her life. All her prayers were answered in Allen, and that made Nyssa begin to cry. She knew that God had been too good to her. Yes, she had HIV, but she was still otherwise healthy, stunningly beautiful, had a wonderful career, and a support system like none other. She had not lacked for anything, and she had access to state-of-the-art facilities to fight HIV. As a matter of fact, she had been part of a new testing study that took her HIV-free immune cells and attached HIV fighting antibodies on them to create more HIV-free cells. They were made to fight and take the place of the diseased cells in her body. So, she had been sending her blood samples to Swaziland to be tested along with other subjects that were a part of the new testing regimen. She was on a new HIV drug that worked well with her body as her T-cell count was rising. The goal was to get the numbers to be near normal. There were 1.2 million people infected with HIV in American alone that would love to be part of this testing. She got it for free because of her status as a doctor and because of the hospital she worked at. Her days of having a pity-party were long gone, and she knew she better not ever fix her face to complain again about her situation.

"Allen, I promise to be all you want and even more. I will not let your desire to be with me be in vain. I will do all I can to fight this disease, but I will do even more to give you the same love you are giving me, and then some. I couldn't see how blessed I truly am. I had to go through the heartache and pain of past dates and relationships so I could appreciate you even more. I look forward to seeing you every morning for nasty coffee and daydreaming about us having a life together. To hear what you said to me, I would be a fool to think any other way about you," Nyssa said as tears ran down her face. She wanted Allen to see them because she wanted him to know she truly meant what she just said.

"We will make the most of this relationship, and we will fight HIV together. Think about where we would be right now if last Friday never happened. We would both still be living a lie." Allen got up and walked to the hut to get some napkins. He returned and gently wiped the tears from Nyssa's face. Such a caring gesture warmed her heart.

"I am going to tell you where we would be right now. You would still be begging me to go out with you. That much we know for sure." Nyssa joked, trying to get her tears under control.

"Oh yeah, and stalking you too."

"Right, because Allen, you do have those stalker tendencies. As a matter of fact, you have stalker eyes. You know those beady eyes you have. Those Peeping Tom eyes that make everyone think you are a creeper. That fits you perfectly," Nyssa said, giving Allen a kiss on the lips.

"I would definitely stalk you. Fine as you are, I would."

Nyssa loved when Allen complimented her. There were only two other men in her life that complimented her—her father and Mr. Manzini. Just thinking of Mr. Manzini reminded Nyssa of a question she wanted to ask Allen.

"Allen, I need a huge favor from you. The Swaziland HIV Foundation in Africa is having a 30th anniversary celebration in six months, and they have invited me to go, but I want you to come with me. I asked Rachel, but she isn't able to go. I don't think I can handle being back at the place of my accident without some support."

"Of course, I will go. I want to be a part of this too, so I will do what I have to do to go."

"Thank you, Allen, that means so much to me. I

miss Swaziland, and it's been too long since I have been there. That is my ministry, and I let my self-loathing take away what God gave me as my ministry. Those children mean everything to me, so I am excited that you are coming with me." Nyssa did a little happy dance on the inside. She was getting those old butterflies back; the same ones she got when she used to travel to Swaziland. She missed the people that worked and lived there. She missed the food and the great feeling she felt at the Foundation when she was there working. She knew other feelings would pop up, but she felt better knowing that Allen would be right by her side.

"Nyssa, for the rest of day, let me show you what our lives will be like if we stay together." Allen reached over and grabbed Nyssa's hand.

"I hope there is some shopping, because I need some new stuff."

"That is a negative, but I hope you will settle for spending quality time together." Allen kissed the back of Nyssa's hand. Nyssa just sat there looking over the water. She knew she was where her heart was content. At this very moment, sitting with Allen, her heart no longer hurt for love. Her heart was no longer suffering disappointment and failure. Her heart was getting stronger because it fed off the love she had for Allen. She wanted this feeling all the time, but knew she would have to be the best Nyssa she could be to stay positive about what she was dealing with. She didn't care about what it took, because at the moment, the only thing she could think about was this great place and the new love of her life.

"Let's enjoy this water while we are here."

"I was thinking the same thing," Nyssa agreed as she stood up and began walking towards the water.

"I am not going to lie…you look good in that two-piece swimsuit. I was expecting you to come out in a one piece," Allen said, catching up to her.

"Consider yourself lucky that I am showing you any skin at all. I just thought that maybe I would give you another reason to be with me." Nyssa winked Allen.

"I didn't need any other reason to be with you. I would have wanted to be with you no matter what, but you're right, it does help a little though." Allen said smiling. Nyssa couldn't help but to smile back. Allen made her feel so special, and she loved it. "Hey, I have an idea. Let's get on this raft." Allen pointed to a raft with a palm tree standing on it. "You grab our teas, and I will pull the raft into the water, then we can get on it." Allen took the raft to the water's edge and stood next to it to wait for Nyssa to come to him. "Okay, you get on, and I'm going to push it out further in the water, then jump on it."

Allen grabbed onto Nyssa's arm to help her get on the raft. Nyssa walked to where the palm tree was standing up and sat down next to it. She watched Allen push the raft out over the water and climb on. He walked towards her, and sat down. He leaned his back against the tree, motioning for Nyssa to sit closer. She obliged and slid towards him, leaning against Allen's body for support. She set the tea down behind them on the other side of the tree.

"This raft is nice and cozy."

"It is. It's like a floating oasis."

"That's true. A love oasis," Nyssa said as she grabbed Allen's hand again. Allen looked deeply into her eyes and gave her a flirtatious wink. Nyssa loved that spark in his eye, because it made her feel like nothing else mattered besides her. Allen leaned in and kissed Nyssa. So, soft and so sweet, was all she could think of. Nyssa laid on her back. Allen did the same thing next to her. Nyssa looked up and admired the beautiful blue sky above them. There were only a few clouds and a nice little breeze. The sun was shining down on their bodies, and it felt so relaxing. This was truly a floating oasis.

Nyssa loved how a simple raft made life not seem so bad. The raft just drifted out, and they held hands as they quietly enjoyed the view. Nyssa didn't know what Allen was thinking at the moment, but she knew she was feeling perfectly content. Laying there, floating on the raft, was such a release. This was a welcome break from the norm. She didn't even know of this place, but she knew it wouldn't be her last time coming here. She wanted this to be one of their regular places to hang at. Nyssa wasn't proud of everything that led up to bearing her soul to Allen, but she was happy they'd made it through, and that they were closer than ever. Now that she could be herself, she knew this relationship would take off like a rocket—that she could count on. Nyssa closed her eyes and drifted off to a place of bliss.

6

"Oh my, this red velvet cake is so moist and delicious," Nyssa commented as she enjoyed a piece of cake from Allen's coffee shop.

"You were right, Nyssa. This cake is the best. I'm not big on sweets, but this cake is making me change my mind about that," Nyssa's father said as he savored another bite.

"I told you! That's why I said we didn't need to get any dessert at dinner."

"But you love the cake at our favorite restaurant. We have gone there every month since you were a little girl, and you swore by the desserts there."

"You're right, but Dad, once I tasted these cakes here, I knew I wouldn't want dessert from anywhere else. Every variety I have tried here have been excellent."

"Allen really knows what he is doing. His coffee is

the best around, and he bakes as well… impressive."

"No Dad, he doesn't bake. He gets them from a bakery in Dallas called 'Sweet Treasures Bakeshop.' The owner, Leah Washington, is well-known for her cakes, and her cupcakes as well. So, I am just letting you know, for all occasions, this is where you need to get our desserts from. Just throwing it out there," Nyssa said as she finished off her cake.

"Duly noted."

"Dad, was there a particular reason why you wanted to come here tonight? Usually after we eat our dinner, you are ready to go home and get some sleep. It is already past your bedtime, so what gives?" Whatever he wanted to talk about, he could have said at the restaurant.

"Yes, there is," her father answered as he looked down at his empty plate. It was something about his demeanor that made Nyssa feel like he was about to drop a bombshell on her.

"C'mon Dad, what is it?"

"Nyssa, I am so happy that you are at a place of peace. Over the past five months, you have been the Nyssa of old. You are happy, energetic, and content with your situation. I know it all stemmed from when you finally came out and told Allen the truth about your health, and I get that. That took a lot of courage to do, regardless of how you were forced to do it. What matters most is that you got it off your chest and that had to have helped you emotionally."

"It did dad. A huge weight was lifted that night I finally talked to Allen about everything, and his response was a blessing. I have thanked God for that."

"That's what I'm talking about. God has opened your eyes to His plan for your life. You were fighting it at first, but now you realize that. I believe that's what made it so easy for you. You let go of the anger you had with God. You were so mad and upset at Him that you couldn't fully see what He was doing in your life. All the while you focused on the one bad thing, and even though it was major, you put all your time and effort into thinking about it."

"I did Dad, and I was so miserable every day because of it," Nyssa agreed, thinking back to the three years of despair. She had been so mad at God that it was hard to even think of Him without thinking negatively about Him.

"I know baby, and once you released that anger towards God, the devil no longer had that thorn in your side to compel you to rebel. You took away what he was using to separate you from God, and you overcame that, and I am proud of you. It took a lot to admit that you had anger against God and to apologize and move on. That shows spiritual maturity, and that was all I ever tried to instill in you."

"I know Dad. You always made sure I was equipped spiritually to face any test given to me. I had my feelings dialed up to one hundred, and I became a selfish wreck. That's what bothered me the most. The selfish part really tore me up because that was so much like Cathy. She was selfish, running out on us like that and never coming back. What type of mom would do that? How could someone turn their back on their marriage and child and just disappear? You see it's making me mad just thinking about it." Nyssa could feel her blood pressure rising. Anytime she talked about her mom, she could feel it changing her whole mood. She didn't like how it made her feel, so she avoided most conversations about her mom. Only her father would bring her up. Nyssa should have known this was why he wanted to talk to her.

"Well… about your mom," Her father began as Emily walked up to the table. She was showing her award-winning smile. It was something about Emily that brightened up Nyssa's day every time she saw her. Allen said that it was something, 'spiritually special' about her and that was why she affected everyone like that.

"Hold that thought Dad. Hey Emily, so good to see you!" Nyssa said, standing to give Emily a hug. Emily hugged her back a little tighter than usual. Nyssa already knew that Emily was a great hugger, but it was something different about this hug.

"This handsome man right here is my father, James Thorne."

"Hi Emily," Nyssa's father said as Emily reached down and hugged him, catching him totally by surprise. Nyssa smirked at the awkward look on her father's face.

"She's a hugger," Nyssa said laughing.

"Sorry, but it's true," Emily said, laughing with Nyssa. "I hate to interrupt your conversation, and all but…"

"No worries. Is something wrong?" Nyssa felt like something might be wrong, because normally Emily was straight forward with her conversations. The look of worry on her face was felt by Nyssa and her father as well.

"Here, have a seat," Nyssa's father offered as he pulled up a chair so Emily could sit down. She sat and she began to get teary eyed. Nyssa had never seen any emotion from Emily except joy. This was a first, and Nyssa was a little alarmed about it.

"Emily what's wrong? Is everything okay with you?" Nyssa said as she put her hand on Emily's arm.

"God has put this on my heart to tell you for a while, and I kept putting it off, but He won't let me rest until I tell you."

"Okay, well... what is it?" Nyssa asked, taken aback by that statement. That was the last thing Nyssa thought she would hear from Emily.

"Okay, let me first start off by saying that I admire you so much Nyssa. You are so beautiful, sweet, and all around awesome. Ever since the first time I met you, I knew it was something special about you. The way you carry yourself, the way you treat your clients, and how you are always so nice. I love that about you," Emily said with so much sincerity that Nyssa felt like she was talking about someone else. Nyssa never really wondered how people perceived her, but she made sure she treated them the way she wanted to be treated.

"How sweet of you to say that Emily. That means a lot to me."

"Don't mention it. Allen sat me down one day and told me about your situation. I hope that was okay with you." Emily said as tears formed in her eyes. "I am so sorry Nyssa. I am so sorry for you."

"Don't cry Emily. I'm okay. I gave Allen permission to tell you so you're fine. You are like family to me." Nyssa reached over to hold Emily's hand.

"I feel so bad for you. Once he told me what led up to you getting HIV, I was floored. It took me a long time to get over it. Of all the people to get it, why you? I questioned God about it, I am not going to lie."

"I did too at first, Emily. You can only imagine how I felt. I had to come to the understanding that God had a plan, and even though that plan is what it is, I had to trust God and lean on Him. It's His plan, so why not put my trust in Him so He can be in control, and He gets to keep the responsibility of seeing it through. All I have to do is just watch God work, and that is what I'm doing," Nyssa said with a confidence she'd just found. Over the past five months, her trust in God had grown to a level that she was even surprised at. All she knew was that she didn't want to do anything to hinder what God was doing in her life.

"Wow, that is so awesome to hear. I wish I had that confidence and strength," Emily said as she wiped away a tear that ran down her cheek.

"You do have that Emily. I see it in you, believe me, I do. You inspire me to be the person that I am."

"That is so nice of you to say that, but if you would had met me a few years ago, you wouldn't have said that."

"Don't say that, Emily. Don't give anything that power over you. That is old news, and today is a new day that God has given you."

"Oh, I know and I believe that. I know I am a new creature in Christ, but before I started working here, I was full of troubles. What God has put on my heart to tell you is this… thank you for being my hero and giving me a reason to keep fighting."

"Wait, what did I do, Emily?"

"Let me tell you my story, then you will know what I am talking about. The Emily you see today is not the Emily I used to be. A few years before I started working here, I was hooked on prescription drugs. I received that bad habit from my mom. For as long as I can remember, my mom cared about nothing but the prescription drugs. My father left us because of it. Our family disowned her because of the lying and stealing that went with her addiction. So, it was basically me and her. Still, she never cared about me or my well-being. She would speak to me or hug me when she wanted something. 'I love you' was always backed by a request for prescription drugs. I had almost every mental sickness known to man because she used me as means to get the drugs when the doctors cut her off. So, she told me to lie and say I had this or that mental issue, so she could keep my meds. What could I do? That was my mom.

She couldn't help me with my problems because she never took care of hers. She masked her problems with prescription drugs and figured, if it worked for her, then it should work for me. So, she supplied me with pills every time I came to her with an issue. No matter how small or large the problem was, her fix for it was always prescription drugs. So, of course, I became dependent on them as well. I spent my high school days in a blur of being overly medicated. I can't remember hardly anything about school. Anyway, my mom ended up dying of liver failure because of the abuse. I never got a chance to say goodbye. I was a wreck, and I depended on the prescription drugs even more. I had no way of coping with what was going on in my life so I decided to end it all.

I knew my mom had a gun in her closet for protection. So, I went there and found the case she kept the gun in. I closed the door behind me because my aunt was downstairs. She moved in to take care of me. I sat at the back of the closet, and I slowly opened the case. Even though I wanted to end it all, I was still afraid of guns. I opened the case and there it was. I picked the gun up and there was a note under it. I thought that was strange. I figured it was instructions on how to use a gun or something, so I picked it up and opened it." Emily had tears running down her face. Her lip began to quiver, and she was visibly shaken. Nyssa squeezed her hand even tighter, and her father put his hand on Emily's shoulder, for support.

"The note said, 'Don't do it Stephanie. Remember, you love Emily, and you don't want her to suffer without you. Get a hold of this addiction so you can be the mother you need to be. Please do that for her. Always remember you love her.' It was signed by her and it broke me down. I never felt love from her or thought she even thought twice about me. It was her addiction that caused her to be the person she was. I kept on blaming her when it was partly her fault, but she was never able to get a grip on her addiction. That note told me that, deep down inside, she cared for me, and that was all I had ever wanted to hear. I couldn't see it, I couldn't feel it, but she did, and that was enough to make me put the gun down and face my addiction.

I stopped blaming her for my situation and I forgave her. That helped me move forward, and I started doing all I could to control my addiction. I ended up, by chance, going to a church with a boyfriend of mine. It was there God spoke to me and gave me the strength to shake my addiction. I changed my life, my attitude, and my perspective on everything. I started living for God and doing as Jesus would, and that is who I am today. The part that I thank you for is this... before I knew you had HIV, I wanted to be like you. I could find no happiness in where I am today because as a little girl I wanted to be a doctor or teacher. I felt a strong desire to help others and that was my goal. I expected so much more for my life, but here I am doing what I do now and feeling like I am nothing. I complained and complained to God about the hand I was dealt, and how I deserved better.

Then, here you are dealing with something much worse, yet I saw God in your actions, your smile, the way you carried yourself. I think back over our interaction and conversations over the past ten months and not once did you complain about life or outwardly show a pity-party. You were all love, and that is what I love about you. In the face of one of the worst circumstances, you are still being a blessing to everyone. Your clients love you, I love you, and Allen loves you. You are so blessed, and I am so happy that I met you, because you are my hero and I wanted you to know that. Your strength to live and desire to please others is obvious. I want to encourage you to keep on being who you are, no matter what," Emily professed as she continued to cry. Nyssa stood up and gave Emily a big hug—both crying. Nyssa thought it is funny how she was inspired by Emily because she thought Emily had everything together. Hearing her talk today made Nyssa realize that we are all going through something, but it is how we act in the midst of it that gives people strength to face their own situation.

"Emily, I do love you, and thank you for sharing that. It has been hard for me at times, but God opened my eyes. I'm so glad that I was able to inspire you to carry on." Nyssa looked over at her father, and he was shaking his head in approval.

"I just wanted you to know that. You are my inspiration, and I am so blessed to know you. Okay, I have to get back to work, but thanks for listening to me, and thank you for letting me take some of your time. It was a pleasure meeting you Mr. Thorne." Emily hugged them both and walked off.

"Look at God. He is always working things out, and when we see what He is doing, it blows our mind," Nyssa's father said as he sat back down.

"I love that girl, but I had no clue of her story. I just assumed she was good because she is always so bubbly and loving. To think she thought highly of me to be her inspiration." Nyssa thought about the conversation that just took place. To realize that God was always placing people in our lives for a reason, and that there are no coincidences, was a powerful revelation. God knew that Emily would need some inspiration to continue her walk, and so He placed Nyssa in her life. It was so hard to fathom how deep God truly was.

"That is amazing. What a testimony she has."

"She does have a powerful one. Her mom was addicted, she was addicted, and both had the same desire to end it all. And the same note kept them both from going through with it."

"How powerful is that story? God used that note to spare her life, but did you hear the part she said about even though her mom was part of the cause, she forgave her, and moved on."

"Yes, and that was so Christ-like of her to forgive her mother."

"Yes, it was, but my question to you is, can you?" Nyssa's father asked as he stared at Nyssa. It took Nyssa a second to realize that he was speaking to her about her mom.

"Wait, our situations with our moms are totally different."

"Really, I don't think so. I think Emily felt abandoned by her mom. I know she felt like her mom could have done more to help their situation instead of turning her focus on something else. The sad part is that her mom passed on, but your mom is still here. You still have a chance for redemption in that relationship. Your mom is alive, and I think the best thing for you to do is consider forgiving her so God will heal that wound."

"Is she still alive, Dad? You don't know that. She could be dead or have a brand-new family. Who knows about her these days?" Nyssa said as she felt a little defiant in her stance against her mom.

"Nyssa, I am going to say it just like this. Your happiness is not tied into your relationship with your mom, but will you never be at the place God wants you to be with her unless you forgive her and move on. Will you enjoy the fullness of life knowing that every time you think of her, you get angry, and it becomes a mood killer?" Nyssa felt like, once again, her father was spot on. She knew this was a black cloud over her life. How could she claim to know God and be a witness for Him to strangers when she was willing to disown her own mother and treat her worse than a stranger?

"Uh, you're right Dad. I need to do better with this issue. I need to work on how I feel about her. I don't know about a relationship though, because I wouldn't know what to do or where to start."

"Yes, you do sweetheart. You do and it can start tonight." Nyssa's father smiled at her mischievously.

"Tonight? Like that is going to happen. You must find her and talk her into it like you did me. Good luck with that," Nyssa said shaking her head at the thought of her mom being willing to talk to her. After all the times they tried in the past to get her to at least call Nyssa, how the constant rejection was too much for her to stand growing up; Nyssa promised she would never let her mom let her down again.

"When God wants something to happen, it happens," Nyssa's father said as he motioned behind Nyssa. She turned around to see who he was motioning to—her mom. The first thing Nyssa thought was that she was looking at her twin. She couldn't believe how much they looked alike. Immediately that cliché 'she thought she had seen a ghost', came to her mind as she couldn't believe her mom was now standing in front of her—of all places, inside of Allen's coffee shop. This was Nyssa's sanctuary, and the last thing she wanted was to see her mom here. Nyssa was shocked as she watched her mom walk up. It had been over thirty years since she'd last seen her mom. Nyssa was almost five when her mom left her, so seeing her now felt eerie.

"Hi Cathy," Nyssa's father said as she approached to the table.

"Hi James, thanks for inviting me. Hello Nyssa, you look so beautiful," Cathy said as she smiled genuinely at them.

"Cathy," Nyssa said as the shock of seeing her mom for the first time was still heavy.

"Nyssa…" Nyssa's father said to correct her for not acknowledging Cathy and calling her 'mom'.

"No, James its fine. She could call me a whole lot worse, so Cathy will work just fine." Nyssa felt Cathy just wanted to keep the peace at this moment. It was still a total surprise to see her mom. Never in a million years did she ever think that she would see her again, but deep down inside, she didn't care to anyway. After all the pain that was felt growing up without her, seeing her now didn't bring back any of the feelings she once had for her mom.

"Well ladies, my job is done. I am going home. Nyssa, I will talk to you later. It was good seeing you again, Cathy. Don't be a stranger. Good night ladies." Nyssa's father stood up and gave Cathy a hug. He then walked over to Nyssa and kissed her on the cheek before giving her a hug.

"Make me proud," he whispered in Nyssa's ear as he hugged her. He then turned and walked out of the coffee shop. So now, Nyssa was sitting alone with her mom and the awkwardness was felt by both. Her mom felt like a complete stranger to her. Nyssa didn't feel that there was any connection other than their looks.

"Nyssa, it really is good to see you. I know you have a million and one things you want to say, a million things you could say, and I understand that. All I ask is that you hear me out, then you can say whatever you need to," Cathy began as Nyssa nodded her head in agreement.

Nyssa was fighting anger and disappointment in her mother. She had to remind herself that she was in Allen's coffee shop; therefore, she needed to be on her best behavior for him, and Emily as well. What got to Nyssa was the fact that she never thought this day would come. It never crossed her mind that they might cross paths again. Nyssa had no clue if her mother was even dead or alive, so she never gave it much thought. Now that she was here, Nyssa wondered what she could possibly want to say that would make this situation better.

"I received a call a year ago from James. I don't know how he found me, but he did. I had moved to Florida, and I was staying with a cousin of mine. Anyway, he called and put me on the spot. He made me give him the reasoning behind what I did thirty years ago and why I did it. I had to face the fact that I never gave him the respect that was due to him. He deserved to know, just like you deserve to know. I was open and honest with him. I told him exactly what happened. Time will tell if he forgives me or not, and it will be the same for you."

Nyssa just shook her head in agreement, because in her mind, this talk was thirty years too late. So much could have been done in the past to explain why it all went down, instead of having a child grow up thinking that her mother hated her and didn't want to be around her. Nyssa had her defenses up, so if she was looking for pity or money, then Cathy was barking up the wrong tree.

"I understand if you are mad at me, and probably hate me for what I did, but just hear me out. I am sorry for abandoning you and your father. I know there were ways I could have handled things better, but I didn't, and I must face that. All these years, I've wanted you to know that I have been praying for you and James. I have prayed that you will forgive me and move on passed the disappointing thing I did. No husband or child deserves what I did, but I felt I had to. Let me try to explain to you like I explained to James. Then, decide if you want me in your life as I try to be a part of yours. Well, I do love you and James. You guys were everything to me, and I know with my actions that is hard to believe, but it's true. It hurt it me to the core to leave that night, but I had to."

"Wait, Cathy. You didn't leave at gunpoint or anything like that. You packed your bags and left. You planned it out, and you went through with it. You left me and Dad to pick up the pieces and to wonder what we did to run you off. Dad cried and cried over you. I didn't like seeing him like that, but what could I do? I missed you just as much as he did. At first, he made excuses for you, but after a while, he just stopped trying and didn't mention you anymore. I can tell you this, he never said anything bad about you, and I mean not one time. He wanted to encourage me to hold on, that you would return, but you never did." Nyssa could recall the pain of her mother leaving and the devastation that was left behind as if it happened yesterday. Watching her father cry was hard on her; he was all she had left once her mother walked out.

"You're right. I wasn't forced out or taken against my will. I chose to pack up my things and leave, but believe me when I say that I had to," Cathy said fighting emotions that were rising to the surface.

"You keep on saying that you had to, but you also said you weren't forced against your will. So, what makes you think you had to?" Nyssa asked accusingly. It was like she was purposely trying to fast talk Nyssa into believing that she had no other recourse than to leave.

"Nyssa, I am bi-polar. I have been all my life. Unfortunately, it runs on my side of the family. My mom, her dad, many cousins have struggled with it. I once was on meds, but I didn't like the way they made me feel. I was a shell of myself. I met your father and I fell in love with him. I stopped taking my meds when we first started dating. The love I felt for him made me feel so much better that I didn't even need the meds then. I was enjoying a normal life, but the illness kept on creeping back in and the symptoms returned with a vengeance. I tried to maintain without the meds, but it was too hard. Then, we got pregnant with you. I promised myself that I wouldn't take any medication because I didn't want you affected by them at all. I prayed that you wouldn't be bi-polar. I prayed to God, saying that he could make my bi-polar symptoms twice as tough, just as long as you didn't have it. I was so happy when I was pregnant. I had always wanted a baby. I found out you were a baby girl and I was so ecstatic. That gave me the ability to make it through the pregnancy with no problems at all. As soon as I had you, and I looked in your eyes, I could feel it down in my soul that you wouldn't carry my burdens. I thanked God that he'd spared you, and I see that I was right.

About a month after I had you was when I started to feel postpartum depression. I started having feelings of despair and visions of hurting you. I can be honest now and say that, I loved you one second, and the next second I was fighting the urge to harm you. That went on for the first three years of your life. It went from me feeling that way monthly to weekly, to me feeling like that daily. When it got that bad, I knew I had to go. Between the symptoms of being bi-polar and postpartum depression, I cracked under the pressure. I cried for weeks before I left. I couldn't get my mind under control, and I knew that the urges were getting too strong. So, I decided to just leave. I called my cousin, who knew about our family history. She bought me a ticket, and I was off to Florida," Cathy said, finally letting her tears out.

Nyssa didn't know how to feel because her anger with her mom had been a part of her for so long. A wave of understanding was overtaking the anger, though, as Nyssa could recognize why her mom did what she did. To think that her mom was fighting a daily battle to preserve Nyssa's life was something that Nyssa never thought about. She knew it was hard not to have suicidal thoughts with her situation. She had fought thoughts of taking her own life, so how much harder was it for her mom to not take her baby's life? There is a self-preservation switch in all of us when it comes to harming ourselves. That's why it was usually a chemical imbalance, drug, or alcohol abuse, depression, or life events that cause us to override that switch and take our lives. You have to fight against your own mind because that switch might not be there to stop you from doing the unthinkable. Nyssa knew enough about people who were bi-polar to know that it was a battle lost without meds. So, just the fact that her mom had enough sense to realize that she was the issue, and that she didn't want to hurt anyone, was one thing, but her methods of doing it alone left Nyssa wondering how sincere she was about getting well.

"Why didn't you tell dad? He would have done everything in his power to help."

"I wanted too, but I also knew that he would have wanted me to take the meds. I know he would have asked me to think of you and him, and take the meds to keep our family together. Maybe I would have taken the meds, or maybe I wouldn't have been as consistent, but the one thing I would have never told him were the thoughts I was having about harming you. I wouldn't have told him that because how could we be in the same household when he couldn't fully trust me. I would have to be supervised all the time. I couldn't be left alone with you. I felt like I couldn't truly be your mother living like that, so I chose to just leave. The feelings I had were too strong, and for you to live, I had to go. I am sorry that I felt that way then, but I couldn't help it. I would rather risk our relationship to ensure that you live, than to be at home and wondering if today was going to be the day I do something terrible. So, Nyssa, I am not asking for sympathy. Too much time has gone by for that. No, what I am asking for is a chance to know you. That is all I want. I can still be Cathy and all. You don't have to call me 'mom' or anything like that. I just want you to know that I am on my meds again, and it is a dosage that limits the side effects I was experiencing. So, I am good, and I am getting to a place of normalcy. I do know that I never stopped loving you. It may be too late to be your mom, but I will settle for being a friend," Cathy said as she looked at Nyssa with much humbleness and sincerity in her eyes.

Nyssa started to break down. Where would the anger she felt for her mom get her in life? How would it make her life better? Nyssa knew it wouldn't help her at all. She believed her mom and hearing it from her made Nyssa grateful she did leave. To think... her mom wanted to harm her and fought urges daily. That had to be one of the toughest battles to face as a young mother. Nyssa could respect that aspect of her mom because she had to think that she would probably have done the same thing and left to spare her child's life.

"How long have you been back on your meds?"

"About a year. It was right after your father called me."

"Why then?"

"It was during his phone call that I realized I needed to get back on my meds. It wasn't for me... it was for you."

"What? For me? What do you mean?"

"Your father told me that you needed me in your life. He said that in order for you to fight this battle you are fighting, I needed to be the mom you have always wanted— always needed. He said you were in a bad place and that he was worried about losing you."

Nyssa knew exactly what she was talking about. It was about the time she got embarrassed in that restaurant for disclosing that she had HIV. She felt like life wasn't worth living. She was at a low point and having a mom would have made a huge difference in her life.

"So why did it take you a year to finally come around?"

"Well, for one, I had to get the correct dosage of my medication. It had been so long since I took them that there were more options to choose from. Then, I had to wait to see if they worked. Next, I had to find a place to live out here in Houston."

"Wait, you moved back out here?"

"Yes, I can't help you from Florida. I needed to be here to help you. I might not be the best mom in the world, but I have common sense enough to know that I need to be here with you."

"I appreciate that. I do want you to know that I forgive you for what took place back then. I was a child and that is how children rationalize something, with emotions. I was angry, hurt, disappointed, and sad. As I got older, I thought I would feel better, but it got worse because I never dealt with the anger. I was still harboring the pain I felt from you, and I wouldn't let it go. When I saw you, the first thing I felt was anger because it put me in the mindset of a child. I still feel and deal with this like a child would, but I need to be mature and handle this the way an adult would. Just give me some time to replace this anger with happiness by getting to know you as a mother and a friend. There is so much to catch you up on!"

"I know some things about you already."

"I guess Dad told you an earful. He can't hold water to save his life."

"Oh no, I googled you a long time ago."

"What is up with me not realizing that people can just get on the internet and find things out?" Nyssa said as she started laughing.

"Yes, I had been following you through high school, through college. Hey, I was expecting you to break my track records in college, what happened?"

"I could have, but I was tired of everyone saying how much I looked like you, how much I ran like you. Honestly,

I didn't want anything to do with you, so I quit."

"No, I can understand that. It wasn't like I was anyone someone should aspire to be, so I get that."

"I should not have been that mean, but at least I was able to focus on my studies and become a doctor. So, something good came out of it."

"That is so true. I know it goes without saying, but I am so sorry you have HIV. James told me all about it, and I was crushed to find out. Not what I wanted for my daughter, but I do understand that things happen."

"True, and if you want to look at it this way, if I wouldn't have gotten HIV, you wouldn't have got back on your meds, and you wouldn't be here right now. So, I think God had a plan the whole time."

"Yes, he did. Just know that I am going to do all I can to make up for lost time. I owe you that much and I will stay on my meds. You'll see."

"I believe you. I will be patient with you as well and not expect too much too soon. We can't make it all up in one day, so we will take our time, together."

"I love that. Thanks for having a heart that forgives. You get that from your father, because I can hold a grudge with the best of them."

"Oh no, me too. I see that we have a lot in common besides our looks," Nyssa said, and for the first time, she was okay it. She hated the fact that they looked alike whenever it was stated in the past, but now she wanted to work on this relationship, mend the fences of time, and become a family. Nyssa didn't know what was going to happen with their relationship, but she knew that, if it was to work out, she had to be fully committed to it.

"Hey Nyssa, will you need anything else before we

close?" Emily asked as she walked up and took the cake plates that were still on the table.

"You can just make me the usual. Cathy, do you drink coffee? Would you like something else instead?"

"Sure, just bring me some decaf coffee please."

"Got it. I will be right back." Emily walked off.

"I am sorry for calling you Cathy. I have to get use to you being here so bear with me," Nyssa said, as she felt she needed to attempt to acknowledge her mom for who God made her to be.

"No problem. It is what I made it to be, so I will deal with it."

"I do need to be better because we will never get to a place of healing unless I acknowledge you for who you are. God chose you to be my mom for a reason, so I know He wouldn't make a mistake."

"You're right, but I've made plenty of mistakes. Too many to name, but leaving you was the biggest one. I am so proud of you, and I know James did a better job raising you than I probably could have. You are a doctor, and if it was up to me, you would be in the Olympics running track. Now you know that you broke a string of athletes that runs in my family. Every generation of girls broke the previous record set by a family member. It is what we do."

"Well, maybe I will start a new string of doctors. That way we can have something more to look forward to."

"Okay, let's do that. So, are you saying that children are in your future?"

"Ha-ha, not that I know of. I definitely don't want my child to have HIV, so I might have to adopt, but who knows."

"We will let God sort it out for us," Cathy said as she

smiled. Nyssa felt like she was looking in a mirror.

"Okay, here you ladies go. I do have to ask, though… Nyssa is this your sister?" Emily asked looking back and forth at them.

"Ha-ha no, she is my mom, my beautiful mom," Nyssa smiled with pride at Cathy.

"Wow, I have met both of your parents tonight! That's exciting. I see where you get your looks from. Both of you ladies are beautiful."

"Well, mom this is Emily. She shared her testimony with me earlier, and by her doing that, I can understand what I need to do for us. She has gone through a lot with her own mom, but she chose forgiveness over anger. I listened, and I learned from that. So, thank you, Emily, for sharing because I needed to hear that."

"No problem at all, Nyssa. Well, I am going home now, so I will see you ladies later. It was a pleasure to meet you Cathy," Emily said as she hugged Cathy, then Nyssa.

"What a sweet young lady…" Cathy said as Emily left.

"She is special."

"No, you are special, Nyssa. I have so much regret on time that was missed. Thank you for not treating me harshly for neglecting you."

"One thing I can truly say is that having HIV has humbled me. If I wasn't sick, I probably would have treated you bad and not even spoken to you. I would have unloaded my frustration and anger on you big time. Now, I know better, and I want to be better because I have spent the past three years in and out of a dark place. God has opened my eyes, and I will make the best of all situations from here on out. It has been too much pity and too much sadness for me.

I want to get the most out of my life and that starts with you. I want to know you so I can see how much of you is in me. All these years of not having a mother was hard, but you are here now so we can do this," Nyssa said as she gave her mother a hug.

Nyssa just held on to her, because in her mind, this was the first hug she had ever received from her mother. She once wondered what it would have been like to remember anything good from her childhood with regards to her mom. All the memories she had of her were lumped together in that one night she left and never came back. Now, she had the opportunity to make new memories, and Nyssa hoped her mother was back for good.

Nyssa closed her eyes and pictured herself as a little girl hugging her mommy.

Nyssa wondered what life would have been like if her mom hadn't been bi-polar and was able to love Nyssa like a normal mom could. Would there have been days filled with them cooking together, shopping together, and talking about everything? Would they have been best friends? Would they have been more like sisters than mother and daughter? Nyssa didn't know the answer to those questions, but she felt like she was going to have fun getting to know her mother. Nyssa knew God was getting her life's pieces put back together again. She was so happy that things were coming together, and she hoped her life would only get better from this moment forward.

"Hello ladies. I can't have you stay any longer unless you purchase something. Nyssa, you know the rules even though you don't follow any of them," Allen said as he walked up to Nyssa and gave her a kiss.

"Cathy, um... Mom. This is Allen, and Allen this is

my Mom," Nyssa said as she held Allen's hand.

"I know. I met her already. Your Dad brought her in here a few weeks ago."

"Really, my Dad did that and didn't tell me? How in the world are you going to keep a secret from me?" Nyssa said, shocked.

"Really Nyssa? You can't talk at all about keeping secrets," Allen said laughing at her.

"My bad, but that is the past though. You keep one more secret from me, and I will cut you passed the white meat. I am talking about all the way to the marrow, the bone marrow."

"James brought me here because he wanted to show me the place we were going to meet. While we were here, he introduced me to Allen, and I was impressed. He has a few of the same characteristics as your father."

"Yes, he does. He thinks he knows it all, and he dresses just as corny as Dad does."

"That's called style, so don't hate. I am glad to see the two of you talking peacefully. I was worried when your Dad said he wanted to meet here. I wasn't sure how you would react to seeing your Mom, especially after all the things that took place, and how you felt about it. Besides, you need to work on your anger issues."

"Don't worry, I'm going to get you, Allen. Just when you turn your back, I'm going to cut you good," Nyssa said as she pretended to stab Allen.

"Cutting our men runs in the family too. Nyssa, you are more like me than you realize," Cathy laughed, giving Nyssa a high-five.

"On that note, ladies let's go. Cathy, I will drop you off," Allen offered.

"The devil is a lie. I will take my Mom home, thank you."

"Okay then. You take your Mom and call me when you make it home so I know you made it safely." Allen was so impressed with how Nyssa was reacting to her Mom being there.

"Thank you for everything, Allen," Cathy said giving him a hug.

"No problem. You made the most wonderful woman in the whole wide world, and I owe you big time for that."

"No, you owe me for settling for you and not finding someone in my weight class."

"Nyssa, be nice to Allen. He is so sweet," Cathy playfully scolded her.

"I am glad you are here, Cathy, because she does this all the time. She is out of control."

"You love me."

"Well, sometimes," Allen answered as he wrapped his arms around Nyssa in a big hug. He made sure they made it safely to Nyssa's car and opened the door for Cathy to get in. Then, he walked around to the driver side and opened the door for Nyssa.

"Bye bighead," Nyssa said as she gave Allen a quick kiss.

"Bye Miss Thorne." Allen watched her start the car and waved as they drove off.

7

Nyssa didn't understand why she had awakened in her favorite white pajamas in the middle of a street. The scorching sun had her sweating so bad, she was feeling very uncomfortable. The last thing she remembered was laying in her hotel room. She had stayed up late playing dominoes with Allen because she couldn't sleep. They were jetlagged from of the eighteen-hour flight to Swaziland, but sleep escaped them. Nyssa was too nervous about going back to the HIV Foundation. She was having anxiety thinking about it.

Nyssa sat up and tried to put the pieces of last night together. It was eerie because she couldn't hear a sound. Not a car, not a person, not an animal, not even the wind. It was so silent that Nyssa felt like she might be deaf. She soon felt the familiar sensation of panic coming on. Her heart had started to beat faster; Nyssa could hear it, which gave her the reassurance that she wasn't deaf. She looked in all directions trying to figure out where she was. Where was the hotel? Where was Allen? She was totally alone and it scared her.

She looked up at the sun as it blazed down on her. She looked at the few clouds in the sky; they were dark gray like storm clouds. The clouds were moving closer to her from a distance. Even though she didn't know where she was, she didn't want to just sit in the street, so she decided to pick a direction to walk in. Nyssa knew she didn't want to travel in the direction of the storm clouds, so she looked down the road behind her; it looked clear. She glanced to both sides of the road, but it was nothing but desert sand.

Nyssa stood up and realized that she didn't have shoes on, just white socks. Just as she took her first few steps, she could hear thunder behind her as the clouds continued steadily her way. Where is everybody? She wondered. It felt as if she was on a deserted planet with no sign of life as far as the eye could see. All of a sudden, the thunder was so loud that it shook the ground. Nyssa turned around to look in the direction of the thunder and saw a flash of lightning that struck the ground with a blinding explosion. It scared Nyssa to death! It frightened her so much that she took off running down the street in the opposite direction.

Running as fast as she could, there was no shelter in sight and no one to help her. Nyssa figured that she would just run until she saw a building or a place that she could hide from the lightning storm approaching. The thunder sounded like it was getting closer. It kept on getting louder and louder, and it was shaking the ground. Then, suddenly, it just stopped and everything got quiet again. It was so quiet that Nyssa's feet landing on the road became the only sound she could hear.

Nyssa began to slow down. She looked back one

more time to make sure the clouds weren't gaining on her. She noticed they were still behind her, but moving faster than before. As she looked down the road behind her, she thought she could faintly see something in the road. It looked like water was trickling, as if someone left a hose on. She was hot and sweaty and thought she could use some rain water right about now. She wasn't 100% sure if it was water, because it didn't look like rain had fallen from the clouds. Her curiosity got the best of her, as she began to walk towards the clouds.

Whatever was moving on the road seemed like it was coming her way. Once she was close enough to get a good look, she noticed that whatever it was it wasn't moving like water would; it was different. It was coming closer and closer, and she began to feel like maybe this had been a bad idea. She strained to truly focus on what it was. Suddenly, her eyes grew in terror as she realized the road was covered with spiders. There were all shapes and sizes, and they were moving towards her without hesitation. Nyssa quickly turned and ran as fast as she could.

Even though the spiders were a distance behind her, she couldn't help but feel like they were crawling on her. She slapped all over her body to make sure none were actually there. The horrible thought gave her goosebumps. Nyssa screamed as loud as she could, hoping that someone would hear her. The air began to cool as the storm clouds finally caught her and were right overhead. Nyssa hoped they would release some rain to possibly wash the spiders away.

In this moment, she was glad she was an athlete because she was moving fast. No spiders would be able keep up with her, but she looked back for good measure.

Just as she breathed a sigh of relief, she could feel drops fall from the clouds above. Nyssa welcomed it, as they felt cool on her skin. Nyssa looked down at her feet and noticed some red dots on her socks. She then looked down at her pajamas—more red drops there as well. Nyssa quickly took her hand and wiped her face. Looking at her hand, she noticed there was blood all over. Then, the realization hit her—this wasn't rain falling from the clouds; it was blood. Nyssa began to run as fast as she could, but the faster she ran, the harder it rained blood, until Nyssa was covered in it. She started freaking out because there was nothing she could do to shield herself from it. Nyssa looked down the road in front of her, hoping she was running towards shelter or anything to help her out. She could see what looked like a sign on the side of the road, and that gave Nyssa a small ray of hope. She ran faster until she could make out letters. As she got within range to read the sign, she stopped in her tracks.

The sign read: "Caution HIV Infected Rain. Don't get it on you, or it will get in you!" Suddenly, her feet began to sink into the ground. She was up to her shins and wasn't able to move. The rain began to come down ever harder for about thirty seconds, and then it stopped abruptly. Nyssa was fighting to get her legs out of the road, but it was no use. The blood stopped falling, and she was able to wipe it out of her eyes. She looked behind her and noticed the spiders were still coming—and coming faster than before. Nyssa tried to pick up her legs, or even kick her way through the ground, but she couldn't move. The spiders were so close that she could make out each individual one. They were a few feet from her, and Nyssa's heart was beating right out of her chest. She watched them climbing up her legs. Before they got up to her chest, she screamed at the top of her lungs.

"NO!" Nyssa screamed, sitting up straight in the bed in her hotel room. She jumped up and started slapping all over her body. She ran to the bathroom and turned the light on. She looked herself up and down in the mirror, realizing it was all a nightmare. She was still in her hotel room, and there was no blood or spiders on her. Nyssa took a deep breath as Allen walked into the bathroom.

"You okay Nyssa?" Allen asked, really worried about her.

"I'm good. I had another nightmare," Nyssa said, relieved to see him. She'd felt so alone and abandoned in her dream, so seeing him made her feel safe.

"I could tell you were having a nightmare. You were kicking and swinging. I was snuggling with you one second, and the next second, I was trying to cover up because you were swinging like you were in a street fight." Allen walked over and put his arms around her.

"I'm sorry about that. The nightmare was about spiders and HIV infected blood again."

"Again huh? I hate that. I'm sorry you had to go through that again."

"Yes, and the worst part about it is, in my nightmares, I can't stop myself from being covered in the infected blood, and I can't get away from the spiders. It's that helpless feeling that gets to me every time." Nyssa laid her head on Allen's shoulder as he continued to hug her.

"Is that what you have felt the whole time about HIV? A feeling of helplessness that you have the disease and can't do anything about it?"

"Yes, that's a big part of it. When it was confirmed that I had HIV, I felt like my life was over. I know some of the horror stories first-hand from my studies and definitely from my clients. I knew what I was up against, but I was still scared and that fear made me feel helpless." Nyssa began to cry. "I just want to be healthy again. I hate HIV so much. It has changed the course of my life, and I can't do anything about it. It sucks so much! I try to be strong and put on a good face, but it is still so hard to deal with."

"I know Nyssa. I can only imagine what you are going through. It's okay if you want to cry and say how you feel. Holding it in isn't going to make it better. I'm here for you, and I'm going to do all I can to fight with you every day until we beat this."

"Thank you, Allen. I'm so happy you are here, because without you I don't know if I would still be alive. You have given me a purpose and a new desire to live, and I thank God for you. Only God would make someone like you specifically for me. No one would just choose to be with someone with a deadly disease."

"I know God has a huge hand in this situation, and I can't deny that, but know that it is still my choice. I could have just left you alone after you changed your number and tried to act like you never existed. I could have taken the out that you offered me when we had our heart-to-heart, but I chose to stay. God has always given us the ability to choose right or wrong. I chose to be with you because I love you, and even though HIV is scary, I am not afraid. So, you are wrong when you say no one would choose to be with someone with a deadly disease. I chose you when I first met you. I chose you when I googled you and found out you had HIV. I chose you when you ran off like a clumsy bird. I chose you when you thought I would leave. I choose you now, and I will choose you forever more."

Nyssa thought that was the sweetest thing anyone had ever said to her. No matter how she thought Allen couldn't get any better, he always did something to top what she thought was impossible to top. She saw the genuineness in his eyes, the reassurance in his voice, and felt the love with every touch of his hand. She knew there was a God that loved her beyond measure because of the love Allen gave her. Only God could make a man see passed the disease and love her.

"Allen, I can't thank you enough for being here with me. You are my rock and I love that so much. I will try to keep my whining about HIV to a minimum. I am normally good about not getting sad about it, but that nightmare just had me shook up."

"I understand. I am here for you, so I understand that whining comes with the territory. Your father told me that you might have been the whiniest child in the whole world," Allen said trying to get a smile out of her.

"Alright watch yourself. You thought I was sleep when I was kicking and punching you. Nope, I was wide awake and you are lucky I didn't connect with any of my haymakers because it would have been lights out for you," Nyssa said, starting to feel like herself again.

"You ready to lay back down?"

"Yes, I am. We have a few more hours before we have to go to the Foundation." Nyssa grabbed Allen's hand as they walked out of the bathroom. Allen turned the bathroom light off as they climbed back into their hotel bed. Allen laid behind Nyssa and put his arms around her, holding her tight. Nyssa felt safe, content, and loved. And it was that thought that helped her go back to sleep.

"Hi, Mr. Manzini. Yes, we are ready to go. Okay, the driver is downstairs. Okay, we will see you soon," Nyssa said as she hung up the hotel room phone. It was all about to become a reality for her. She took a deep breath and closed her eyes. She knew that, in no time, she would be at the Foundation for the first time in almost four years. She was happy to be visiting the Foundation again, but still felt nervous. She didn't know the type of response she would get from the workers there. She used to visit and always had encouraging words for them, but the last time she was there she was a doctor; now she was a client.

All morning her stomach was so queasy that she had to force herself to eat some oatmeal and a banana. She had to put something on her stomach. She walked over to the bed and grabbed her purse. She finished putting in all the essentials and took out anything that wasn't necessary for the trip to the Foundation.

"Hey Allen, you ready?" Nyssa asked as Allen walked back into the room from the balcony. She loved the fact that he let her pick his outfit for this celebration. She chose a blue blazer, a white button-down shirt, some dark blue jeans, and gray suede chukka boots. She thought that was a great outfit to match her white dress with dark blue lines down the sides. She wore her hair in her signature bun and just enough makeup to enhance her natural beauty. She normally wasn't big on trying to coordinate with Allen, but she thought it would be a nice touch today.

"I am ready, Sweetheart," Allen said, walking over to her.

"Can you pray for me? I need it," Nyssa asked as she grabbed Allen's hands. She loved his prayers, and she knew he would say exactly what needed to be said. As he was praying, Nyssa had to reign her thoughts in because she was getting even more nervous, and she knew she needed to control it. She didn't know what was going to happen when she got there or what emotions she would feel. She was just trying to prepare her heart and mind for whatever happened.

"Thank you, Allen," Nyssa said as he was finished praying. "Our car is downstairs, so let's go."

Allen nodded his head as he made sure he had the room key in his pocket. He walked over to the balcony and slid the door shut, locking it. He walked over to Nyssa and grabbed her hand as they walked out of the room and down the hallway that lead to the elevator.

"You look outstanding," Allen said, breaking the silence.

"Thank you, Allen. I'm nervous. Sorry that I'm being so quiet," Nyssa apologized.

"I am enjoying you being quiet. It's the first time ever you are not being silly," Allen said trying to get Nyssa to loosen up a little bit.

"Don't press your luck. I am fragile today. I know how to kill you and where to bury you in Swaziland. No one will find you, trust," Nyssa said, welcoming the distraction from her nerves.

As soon as the elevator door opened to the lobby, Nyssa knew she was just a short drive to the Foundation. Allen held Nyssa's hand securely as they walked through the hotel lobby. Déjà vu had come upon Nyssa once again as she felt like she had done this before. It brought back memories for sure. The lobby was exactly the same; it seemed like it had the same people and everything. They went through the rotating glass door that lead to the front of the hotel and were hit with the familiar Swaziland humidity. It was as sunny and bright as always, but Nyssa felt that what made Swaziland so inviting was the pureness of the scenery. Once they made it outside, Nyssa looked around for the gray sedan the Foundation normally used to pick up guests. She didn't see one and began to worry that maybe the car went to the wrong hotel.

As she was looking around, a black limo was parked right in front. It shone like the night sky with chrome five-point rims. The windows had the usual dark tint on them, and the car was extremely clean. However, there were two things that stood out about the car. One, the car had the Swaziland flag sticking up on the hood on the right and left side, as if the car was chauffeuring someone very important. The second thing was a side magnet that had a company logo and motto on it. The company name was, "Movie Star Limos", and the motto stated, "Even you can ride like a movie star."

Nyssa was still looking for a gray sedan. She began to think that maybe this was a sign. The last time she was here, the driver wasn't present to take her to the airport. Maybe something was going to happen again. Nyssa felt paranoia grip her mind and she wanted it to leave as fast as it came.

"What's wrong?" Allen asked as he noticed the look on Nyssa's face.

"I don't see our car," Nyssa explained as she looked around to make sure she didn't overlook it.

"Dr. Movie Star!" When Nyssa heard that name, an

ice-cold shiver traveled down her entire body. "Dr. Movie Star!" the voice called again from an open window on the passenger side of the black limo. The window rolled back up and the driver side door flew open. Out comes Ben, her taxi driver from the day of her accident. He ran around the car similar to the way he had three years ago when he was driving the taxi.

"Ben! What a surprise." Nyssa said. She knew that he had been affected by the events of her last visit just like she was. Not to her extent, but he was still in pretty bad shape afterwards. Ben ran up to her and gave her a hug, laughing the whole time.

"Dr. Movie Star, it is so good to see you."

"You as well Ben. This is Allen Oakley, my boyfriend."

"Hey Boyfriend. Ben wants to know why you haven't married Dr. Movie Star yet. The last time she was here, you was just boyfriend. Three years later, you still haven't made an honest woman of her," Ben said, giving Allen a hard time.

"Hold up, Mr. No Worries. That was a different boyfriend, so slow your roll. This one is a keeper. The last one... not so much."

"No worries, Allen, Ben just giving you a hard time."

"So, I see you are not driving taxis anymore. Good for you."

"Yes, no more taxis for Ben. Since the accident, I quit. I told them Ben no longer work for them. I will work for myself. So, I started my own limo company, Movie Star Limos," Ben said proudly as he walked over to the limo and tapped on the magnet.

"Okay, good for you. Why Movie Star Limos? You could have called it, 'No Worries Limos,'" Nyssa said.

"You are right, I could have called it that. Ben wish he would have thought of that. No, I wanted to name it after you. After what happened, I felt like I had to honor you in some type of way. I heard about what happened at the hospital, and that wasn't right. Ben felt bad because I was driving, and I could have been a better driver for you that day," Ben said, showing a seriousness Nyssa had never seen.

"Oh no, Ben. It wasn't your fault at all. That truck in front of us was at fault. You did all you could that day, and who knows what would have happened if you had hit that safe. Maybe we wouldn't be around to even talk about it today."

"You are right, no worries. So, let's go."

"Wait Ben, the Foundation sent me a car."

"They did and it is Ben. I am taking you to the Foundation."

"Okay…" Nyssa said as she walked over to the limo. Ben opened the door for her. She got in the car and slid over so Allen could get in. Ben's limo was set up a little different than most. Instead of having a long seat in the back and two long seats going up the sides leading to the divider, this limo had one long seat on the left side. It stretched from the divider down the left side and curved at the back, then stopped at the only door you could get in and out of. Just passed the door, on the opposite side, was a bar. It was a two-level marble bar that held empty glasses on the top and the next level had a bin with ice and two bottles of champagne chilling. There was lighting that went across the top of the bar and right under the second level to shine on whatever was there. The rest of the car was lined with small strips of lighting across the very top of the inside. There was a divider that had a small opening in the middle, like most limos do, and there were two twenty-inch televisions on both sides of the small opening.

Ben closed the door and walked to the driver side. He plopped down in his seat and opened the sliding window that separated the driver from his riders. Nyssa liked the look of the interior. It had plush black leather seats. There was a small island in the middle that had more wine glasses hanging all around it. The interior had a black sponge-like material on the top of the inside of the car and along the panels. Nyssa figured it was to make it sound proof.

"Okay, Dr. Movie Star. I have some Malva pudding here for you and your Allen to enjoy," Ben said, handing them a Styrofoam to-go plate through the small opening. Allen grabbed the plate and handed it to Nyssa. Nyssa couldn't help but smile at the gesture. After all, he said she smelled like it and that brought a big smile to her face.

"That is too funny. Thank you, Ben," Nyssa said, opening the plate It looked more like a cake than it did pudding. It looked so moist. Nyssa handed Allen one of the plastic forks and they both took a piece together. Nyssa was surprised at how sweet and fluffy the cake was. It had a distinct taste that Nyssa loved.

"Wow, that is some good cake, or I mean, pudding," Allen said as he went in for another piece.

"Ben wants to know if you like it," Ben said as he pulled away from the hotel.

"Ben, it is awesome. Tell your wife that she is a great cook," Nyssa complimented.

"I will and she will like that."

It was the simple things that Nyssa loved so much

about Swaziland. So much history, so much tradition, and so many good people that just needed a chance. Nyssa knew her heart was missing Swaziland, and now that she was back, she felt whole again. It was something about this place that gave her a calming feeling, and she knew she was back where she belonged—her mind told her that, her heart told her that, her spirit told her that. So much confirmation that Nyssa knew she had made the right choice in finally coming back.

"This place is just as beautiful as you said it was. I am loving how the progress of society hasn't dampened the cultural history at all. You can still see so much tradition in the land, as they have only enhanced life here by modernizing the city. I can see why you love it so much, and I have only been here a few days. I want to come back with you from here on out," Allen said, watching Nyssa who was staring out the window.

Nyssa heard him, but she was so focused on the scenery that she didn't even realize she hadn't acknowledged his statement. She knew the spot of the accident was almost near. She stared more closely out the window, looking for any landmarks she remembered. Her heart started to beat a touch faster. She was about to revisit the spot where her life was changed forever. She knew this was part of the reason why she never wanted to come back to Swaziland. She knew that if she left the hotel, she would have to go by that spot and face it again. At least today, she had Allen with her, and she was even happy that Ben was there as well. After all, he was a part of what took place, and he was part of her memory.

"Dr. Movie Star, we are almost to the place of the accident. Ben wants to know if it is okay with you that I stop and show you something when we are there. It will only take a moment."

"Sure Ben, I don't see any problem with that," Nyssa said even though she wasn't sure it was a good idea.

"Good girl," Allen said reassuringly.

"Maybe we need to open that bottle of wine. I need something to drink."

"Really Nyssa? No, the last time you needed some wine you ran off and left me. You can run off now if you want too, but I will not chase you. It is too hot for that." Allen got a smile from Nyssa, and that was all he wanted. "Let's just get one of these waters." He grabbed a bottled water, opened the top, and handed it to her. Nyssa took a few sips as she kept her gaze out the window.

To the people of Swaziland, this road was a lifeline to the hotels, corporations, hospitals, airlines, and the Foundation. But, to Nyssa, this road lead to memories that she had nightmares about. So many Africans used this road as way to make a living, but Nyssa saw the road as a way to her destruction. She might not care about it as much, and if it was up to her, she wished it wasn't there, but to the people that truly counted on it, it was the one thing kept some of them alive.

All of a sudden, the limo started to slow down, causing Nyssa's heart to speed up. Flashbacks of her bleeding, hurt, and being afraid that she might not make it replayed themselves in her mind. The limo slowly came to a complete stop. Ben got out of the driver seat and walked around to open the door. Allen looked at Nyssa and nodded to let her know she would be okay. Ben opened the door, and Allen slid down the seat to get out, then held his hand out so Nyssa could get out. She stood up and looked around. Nothing was as it once was. You couldn't tell anything happened at that spot, as it looked like any other part of the road. Nyssa looked down the road in the direction they were traveling. She could see the Foundation in the distance.

"Come around here, Dr. Movie Star," Ben said. "About twenty yards down the road there was where we hit the other car." Ben pointed in the direction they had been headed. "We flipped over about a half a dozen times and the spot where we landed is over here." He walked to an area about five-feet from where they had parked. There was a small twenty-inch wooden cross sticking out of the ground. It had tons of ribbons tied to it. There were a few weather-worn stuffed animals and a stethoscope as well.

As they got closer to the cross, Nyssa noticed that there was a small metal plate with writing on it. Ben crouched down next to it—Nyssa and Allen followed. Nyssa was now close enough to see what was written on the small metal plate. It said: "Here is the spot a great doctor was taken from us." As soon as Nyssa read the message, tears formed in her eyes. She felt like there wasn't a truer statement than that.

This spot had taken her away from them. Because of what happened here, Nyssa had never been the same. It took her desire to return away. It took her desire to do God's will away. It almost took her desire to live away. Allen put his arm around Nyssa as she broke down and cried. She felt so much remorse. She felt like she let everyone down. Year after year, she was here telling everyone that everything was going to be okay. She came with money, she came with medicine, and she came healthy. As she was administering vaccines and treatments. She would say over and over again that HIV wasn't the end of the world and that they still had so much to live for. Yet, when the shoes were on her feet, she didn't believe it—she allowed herself to be crippled by it. When HIV found her home and invaded her life, it was as if the world was over and that was the polar opposite of what she told the sick ones at the Foundation, and her clients back in Texas. It was so easy to encourage when you were the encourager, but when the encourager needed encouragement, it was a whole new ball game. Nyssa knew she didn't display half the courage or will to live as the people she had helped. She stood here now, realizing her mistakes, knowing she had work to do in order to be where God wanted her to be.

"I understand why they wrote that. I was dead."

"I wrote that. I wrote that on behalf of the children that I have seen over the years. That is what they tell me has happened. I told them it wasn't true, and that you would be back one day. So, I made sure that I marked this spot with a cross, because it was no one but God that saved our lives that day. We had no reason to walk away from that crash. I was going at least sixty miles an hour when we hit that car about as solid as you possibly can. We flipped over and over again and ended up on all four tires. Ben wasn't a religious man then, but I am now. Ben knows that God was watching over us that day, and no one can tell me anything different.

You see, Dr. Movie Star, those children told me they loved you. They missed you, and they felt this accident took you from them because you never came back. They blamed this accident for why you stopped coming. Ben told them that you will return. Ben felt that because I remember you saying you love making a difference in other peoples' lives. Ben knew you wouldn't turn your back on those children, and I was right. I tell you this much, Ben comes out here every Friday, and I pray at this spot. I pray for Ben, I pray for Susan, and I pray for you. Now that you are here, Ben thinks I can let it go."

"Because it no longer has a hold on you. I am here and that was the whole purpose of your prayers," Nyssa said, nodding in agreement.

"Right and it shouldn't have a hold on you anymore either. Ben was watching you as we were driving here, and I noticed you were looking intently for something. The Holy Spirit told me what it was, and that is why I decided to stop so we both could be healed."

"Wow, that is definitely God at work." Allen leaned down to get a closer look at the cross. Nyssa felt that was what she needed to hear. She had been so worried about this spot and how it would remind her of getting HIV. Now, she knew this place would remind her of when she let go of the past. Nyssa felt she had overcome her fear and let go of that baggage.

"You're right Ben, let's pull up this cross because I am here, and I won't let anything take me away again." Nyssa put a gentle hand on Ben's shoulder. Ben grabbed the cross and pulled it out of the ground with one strong yank. He walked over to his trunk and placed it inside.

"So proud of you Nyssa, for facing this. I know you were so afraid and your nightmares confirmed that. This is now a figment of your imagination and it has no hold on you anymore. You get to be the person you know you can be. You can get your ministry going again," Allen said.

"You are so right. I am free from this accident. Thank you, Jesus."

"C'mon guys, we are running behind. We have a celebration to attend," Ben said as he tapped the top of the limo.

Nyssa looked over at the spot one more time. She was glad she came out here to face this. Just the fear of what took place here had her terrified of coming back. That was what she felt, but now she felt like it was old news. She knew she would be back again and would pass this spot like it was never there.

Nyssa walked back to the limo as Allen stood waiting on her. He smiled as she climbed in. Ben looked back through the small opening to make sure both were in the limo. They resumed travelling towards the Foundation. Nyssa was beginning to get excited. She was finally able to enjoy being back in Swaziland. Her anxiety and fears were gone, and now she couldn't wait to get to the Foundation. The closer they got, the more butterflies fluttered around in her stomach.

Nyssa looked out the window at the area across the street from the Foundation and could see that the city had grown a little in the last three years. That meant the untouched native land had shrunk. Nyssa understood that this was a part of growth, and if Swaziland was going to attract tourists, they had to adapt to the times. But still, it saddened her that she would one day visit and it would no longer be nature to look at; it would be buildings and corporations. That meant many tribes would have to move further and further out until they had nowhere else to go. Then, they would disappear like many of their elders. That was the fact of the matter of living like the generation before you. As much as it was historical to hold on to things of the past, it also hindered you from reaching your full potential in some cases. As soon as they pulled into the driveway, Nyssa felt like a kid at a candy store.

As the limo came to stop. Mr. Manzini walked out

the front door in a green blazer and khaki pants. Nyssa's heart leaped at the sight of him. He still had that smile that warmed her every time he flashed it. He walked over to the sidewalk and waited for Ben to get out. He gave Ben a high-five before he opened the door for Allen and Nyssa.

"Dr. Thorne, as I live and breathe, it is so good to see you again," Mr. Manzini said as he hugged Nyssa with the warmest of hugs. Nyssa didn't want to let him go. She was so happy to see him again. She missed coming out here to have their face-to-face and heart-to-heart talks. He was so knowledgeable about life and situations, she always learned something new about HIV from him. She felt that she had gained more knowledge from him than all her years in college.

"Mr. Manzini, I am so happy to see you. I can't tell you how much I missed you."

"The feeling is mutual. I have talked about you so much these past three years that I am sure everyone here is sick of it. This here must be Mr. Allen Oakley." Mr. Manzini shook Allen's hand.

"Mr. Manzini, I have heard so much good stuff about you. I am not sure that I can compete with all I've heard."

"Allen, there is no competition here. Just take care of my professional daughter and everything will be fine."

"Oh, he is doing that and some. He is all I have told you and more."

"Good, let's get inside. Everyone is waiting to see you again," Mr. Manzini said ushering them through the door. As soon as the automatic doors opened, a group of Foundation workers quickly came up to greet her. There must have been around thirty ladies that surrounded her with a group hug before they began to get their individual ones.

Ben walked up to Allen. Allen stood a few feet behind Nyssa's welcoming committee. Ben put his arm on Allen's shoulder.

"See I told you, that's Dr. Movie Star."

"Ben, you might be right," Allen agreed.

Nyssa enjoyed the welcome the workers gave her. She knew that all the years of treating them with respect and loving on them made them feel a connection with her. As she was speaking with and hugging the ladies, she truly felt accepted and loved by them. She felt happiness from the inside out. Once Nyssa was done hugging them all, she followed them into the Foundation lobby. The whole place was decorated in green and gold. All the workers had on green tops and khaki bottoms. They went all out for the thirty-year anniversary. There were green balloons and streamers hanging from the ceiling. There were signs and a couple of large banners that said, "Congratulations on 30 Years!" and another one that had, "13 is only the beginning". There was a table that had a large green cake that said the same thing, and another table with a few bowls of green punch.

"Dr. Thorne, welcome back!" Susan said as she walked up with her noticeable limp.

"Susan, oh my. It is so good to see you again." Nyssa gave her a hug.

"Thank you, Dr. Thorne. You look so beautiful. How do you feel?"

"I am good, real good."

"It is a pleasure to see you. I was so worried that I would not be able to see you again. I just want to tell you that I am so sorry for what happened. To think that you would be the one dealt the worst hand. You are so brave, and I know you will fight like the dickens to beat this, I know you will."

"I will fight with everything I got, Susan."

"Dr. Thorne!!!" A group of children ran up to Nyssa and embraced her in a sea of tiny arms. Nyssa was ecstatic to see the children. She missed the love they gave her when she visited. Just about every kid wanted a hug from Nyssa, and they all waited their turn. There was another large group of children that were watching through the window. They were all waving and showing an excitement that made Nyssa feel so valued. Worker after worker walked up to her and let her know that she had been missed, and they were glad she was back. It was a homecoming of sorts. She felt right at home, even though she had been gone for three years. Nyssa felt like she should have kept coming all along because she was drawing on their love for strength. The way she felt now, she would come just for the love and support she was getting.

"Nyssa, you can catch up with everyone later. We need to get our celebration started. So, follow me into the Big Room," Mr. Manzini stated as he tried to escort her to the room where the main celebration was taking place. The Big Room was the auditorium where all meetings, entertainment, and parties were held. It was also where they let the workers perform for the kids, or vice versa. They would have talent shows, or dance contests to keep the children excited and help get their minds off their sickness. It had a large stage, and just recently, they bought a projector and large screen so the children could watch movies and videos to help entertain them on a daily basis.

They lead Nyssa to the very front row where she sat

down in an open seat. Allen sat next to her. Mr. Manzini and Susan went to a control booth next to the stage. All of a sudden, Nyssa could hear the children coming in. So many children kept screaming her name, and Nyssa made sure she waved and acknowledged each and every one. It took a good twenty minutes to get all the children seated. Once in their places, Nyssa noticed that there were twelve empty seats on the left side of Allen. Suddenly, a group of children and adults walked in the Big Room. All the other kids in the room started to clap and cheer as they made their way in.

The lights suddenly went dim, and the projector screen turned on. The children erupted into another wave of cheers. They ran a promo video for the Foundation. Nyssa remembered this video; she had seen it so many times. Once the video was done playing, the words "13 is only the beginning" was shown on the screen. The children went wild, even the ones sitting on the front row began to jump up and down. Nyssa and Allen were clueless as to what all the excitement was about. Mr. Manzini and Susan walked onto the middle of the stage and spoke about the history of the Foundation. After thirty years, the Foundation had come so far thanks to their tireless efforts in the fight against HIV\AIDS. They celebrated a few breakthroughs every few years to where someone got relief from HIV through medicine and treatments. They had grown to not only treat the sick, but to house and school them as well. Mr. Manzini lead a few cheers himself, and the place went into a frenzy. Mr. Manzini then attempted to quiet the children down.

"Okay, let's bring the workers in here," Mr. Manzini announced. He waited a few minutes for the workers to file into the room. "Okay, Nyssa, can you join me and Susan on the stage?" Mr. Manzini asked. Everyone's voice in the room could be heard yelling her name in encouragement. Nyssa walked onto the stage where Susan and Mr. Manzini were standing. Mr. Manzini quieted the crowd once again.

"Our motto is '13 is only the beginning', and it will be that way until we move forward. It has been a great time for the Foundation as we are doing things that the world isn't ready for. We have done our due diligence on the results, tests, and equations. We have tested, retested, and retested the numbers and facts don't lie. '13 is only the beginning' is more than a motto. It truly is the beginning. Thirteen represents the thirteen people that have shown a breakthrough like no others. With the testing procedure we have in place, over the past year, we have been able to afford to test six thousand subjects. This past year we have focused these new treatments on the participants. Out of the six thousand subjects, only thirteen showed a breakthrough, and I am proud to say that as of the last test—a month ago—they are HIV free!" The room went haywire with workers and children running around acting crazy with excitement.

This news was nothing short of a miracle. Nyssa was shocked to hear this, and was so happy for the thirteen subjects that had received the blessing of being healed. She was ecstatic because this breakthrough gave her hope for the future. She was blown away that they were healed, and she believed God could do that for her as well. To know that the Foundation was doing all they could to reassure her that her work at the Foundation wasn't in vain warmed her heart and made her feel like a widespread wiping out of HIV was just around the corner. If someone didn't think thirteen was a lot, they could ask the thirteen for themselves what the big deal was. Those thirteen would tell them that they wanted to be part of the thirteen, and not a part of the millions that were still sick.

"Let's meet the thirteen now," Mr. Manzini said as the children and adults that were in the front room, got up and walked onto the stage. Nyssa hugged each one of them to show how truly happy she was for their miracle. Tears formed in her eyes as she realized that half of them had been born with HIV. Therefore, they were getting their first chance at living a normal life. The other half received it from less than desirable ways, and even though it was sad, Nyssa was happy they could experience life again as they once knew it.

"We know we will still have to do more testing, but we will do all we can to ensure that this breakthrough is permanent!" Mr. Manzini said, encouraging more cheers from the crowd. Nyssa was warmed to see the crowd being so supportive. What a humbling display of love from those who still had HIV. Even though they were still within their own struggle, they could be happy for the ones that were now free from it. No signs of jealousy, only hope that they could be the next ones to have a breakthrough. She looked at Allen and could see that he had a perplexed look on his face; he seemed confused.

"Susan, come over here by me. Nyssa, I need you to do something for me." Mr. Manzini grabbed a packet from the sound booth. "Dr. Thorne, can you pin these numbers on the thirteen?"

"I would be honored to pin it on them." Nyssa was more than willing to help celebrate these thirteen blessed ones.

"As she pins the number on them, I want the crowd to call it out please." Mr. Manzini requested before Nyssa began. Nyssa made her way over to the first person and pinned a #1 on her shirt. The crowd yelled, "Number ONE!" in response. She progressed down the line, pinning numbers two through twelve on each of the miracles standing before her, with the crown playing along the whole way. Nyssa looked around, but there wasn't anyone else to pin the #13 on. Nyssa approached Mr. Manzini with a confused look on her face. She tried to hand him the #13, but he wouldn't accept it.

"Nyssa, count again. As a matter of fact, let's help her count." Nyssa walked back over to the children and put a hand over every kid until she got to twelve, and again, she was one person short.

"Okay Nyssa, I want you to take the microphone and count one more time." Nyssa pointed to every kid and called their number, frustrated when she found herself at the same result.

"Mr. Manzini, there is no thirtieth person here. I have counted them down, but I still have thirteen in my hand." She looked at Allen. He was sitting, eyes wide with his hand over his mouth. What is going on? She wondered.

"Dr. Thorne, you are the thirtieth person," Mr. Manzini announced as the crowd erupted with ear-splitting cheer. Nyssa couldn't believe what she just heard. She looked at Allen, and he was jumping up and down. Nyssa felt like she was going to faint. She couldn't believe it.

"Are you for real?" Nyssa exclaimed, fighting back tears.

"Dr. Thorne, as I live and breathe, you are HIV free," Mr. Manzini said. Nyssa fell to her knees, crying uncontrollably. Mr. Manzini ran over to her, kneeled down, and put his hand on her back. Susan rushed over and did the same.

"Thank you, Jesus! My God, thank you!" was all Nyssa could say over and over. She felt so overwhelmed with emotion. She couldn't move or do anything, but thank God repeatedly. Her tears were flowing down her face, and she wanted to do nothing else but thank God for all he had done. Allen ran on the stage and held her tight. Nyssa bear hugged him close. She knew that she was so blessed to have everything work out for her good, especially after the anger, disbelief, and total disobedience she showed God. God loved her enough to give her something people go their whole lives without receiving—healing.

"I love you Allen. I love you so much," Nyssa cried. She could still hear the kids and workers screaming in the auditorium. Allen had tears in his eyes as well; he could only shake his head in agreement.

"Ms. Thorne, I love you more." Allen helped Nyssa to her feet as the children started chanting her name.

"Dr. Thorne!"

"Dr. Thorne!"

Nyssa looked out at the auditorium, at everyone chanting her name, and at this moment, she realized how precious life was and that God was still in control. The other twelve ran up to Nyssa and hugged her, beginning a new chant of, "13 is only the beginning! 13 is only the beginning!"

Mr. Manzini got on the microphone and quieted everyone down so they could hear what Nyssa and the twelve were chanting. He put the microphone near them, and as they huddled up together, they all chanted into the microphone.

"13 is only the beginning!"

"13 is only the beginning!"

Soon, the whole auditorium was chanting. It was a truly powerful moment. A whole auditorium of people that believed what they were saying; and thirteen that knew it for certain. Nyssa swore she could feel the walls shaking from all the yelling. It was so beautiful to know that the hope everyone had was intoxicating. So, Nyssa kept on chanting as she looked over at Allen, who was still wiping the tears out of his eyes. It was enough to make her get emotional to see him so happy for her. All his talks, prayers, and support for her was enough to make her feel she would forever be indebted to him. He was the beginning of her realizing that God was working her situation out for her good, and he had been all she needed at this crucial moment in her life. Nyssa looked up towards the sky and closed her eyes. She let the chant take her to a place of happiness.

Nyssa had been sitting on her balcony for the past hour, just staring at the water. It was so calm, so peaceful, and she knew it represented her. Seven months ago, she stood on that Foundation stage in Africa and was given a clean bill of health. She had never cried the way she cried that day. Not when her mom left. Not when she quit the track team from the pressure of beating her mom's records. Not when she walked during graduation from med school. Not when she opened her practice. Not when she found out she had HIV. Not when she was embarrassed time and time again for divulging her sickness. Not when Allen accepted her for who she was. Not when her mom came back into her life.

None of those monumental moments were as rewarding, refreshing, fulfilling as that cry was when she realized she was HIV free. Since that day, she has only had a few nightmares, but when she woke up and looked at her last test result, the big letter that read, "Negative", made all things okay again. Even though her blood work was coming back negative for HIV, she still had to get checked out every six months. Nyssa didn't mind. Nyssa and Allen were going to take their relationship to the next level by getting married next summer, and if she remained HIV free for two years, they would plan to have a child.

"Thank you, God, for being so good. I can't thank you enough for blessing me. I promise to honor you with my life, every day," Nyssa said as she thought about how she would always know God was active in taking care of His children. There were so many people who had not been healed, and she knew better than to waste this opportunity God had given her to enjoy a solid win over the enemy. This enemy had its victory in hand, but God changed the outcome. That alone gave Nyssa a quiet peace that would never go away.

All she knew was that she now had a chance to encourage her clients even more, as they had proof that HIV could be conquered. Nyssa was happy that her enemy had been defeated, and now she could bring others to victory. She would lead them to a place where they trusted God more than the medicine. To where they trusted God more than what she told them. To where they loved God as much as God loved them, and if they thought there was no chance for them to beat HIV, they could look to Nyssa's outcome and know they too could beat the enemy inside of them.

Omega

CPSIA information can be obtained
at www.ICGtesting.com
Printed in the USA
FFOW02n0518270917
40375FF